ACCLAIM FOR JEFF SMITH'S

Named an all-time top ten graphic novel by Time *magazine.*

"As sweeping as the 'Lord of the Rings' cycle, but much funnier." —*Andrew Arnold, Time.com*

★*"This is first-class kid lit: exciting, funny, scary, and resonant enough that it will stick with readers for a long time."* —Publishers Weekly, *starred review*

"BONE *is storytelling at its best, full of endearing, flawed characters whose adventures run the gamut from hilarious whimsy . . . to thrilling drama."*
—Entertainment Weekly

"Jeff Smith's cartoons are irresistible. Every gorgeous sweep of his brush speaks volumes."
—*Frank Miller, creator of* Sin City

"Jeff Smith can pace a joke better than almost anyone in comics." —*Neil Gaiman, author of* Coraline

"I love BONE! BONE *is great!"*
—*Matt Groening, creator of* The Simpsons

PRAISE FOR *ROSE*
Prequel to the epic *BONE* saga

"ROSE *is a magnificent prequel to Jeff Smith's* BONE."
—*Neil Gaiman, author of* Coraline

"I love Charles Vess's art so much that I'll buy anything he illustrates, but his collaboration with Jeff Smith on* ROSE *has really upped the ante."
—Charles de Lint, award-winning fantasy writer

"[Vess's] artistry sizzles under his vibrant coloring, which is what really makes the book shine."
—John Hogan, GraphicNovelReporter.com

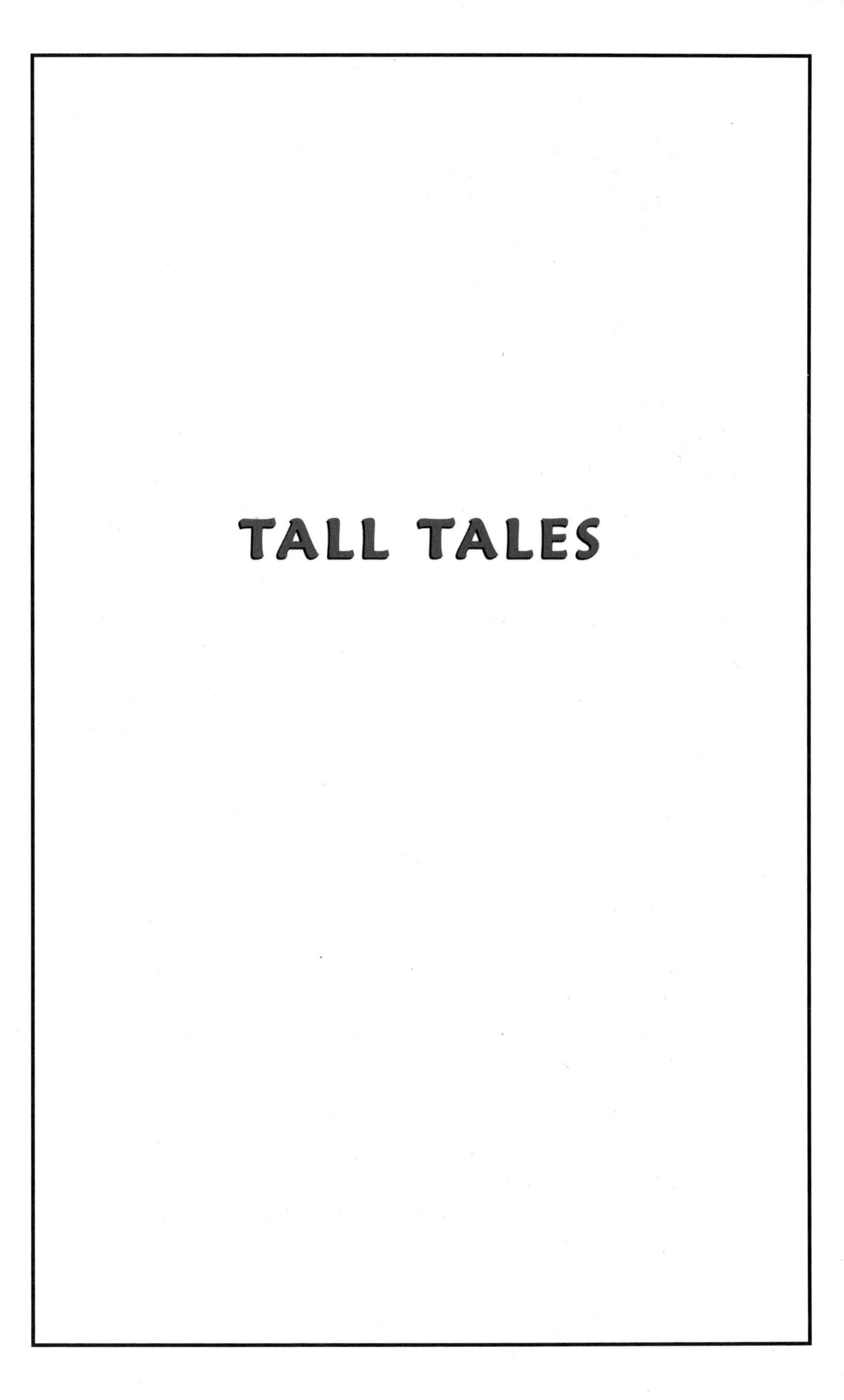

TALL TALES

OTHER ***BONE*** BOOKS

Out from Boneville

The Great Cow Race

Eyes of the Storm

The Dragonslayer

Rock Jaw: Master of the Eastern Border

Old Man's Cave

Ghost Circles

Treasure Hunters

Crown of Horns

Rose (Prequel)

BONE Handbook

TALL TALES

BY JEFF SMITH
WITH TOM SNIEGOSKI

COLOR BY STEVE HAMAKER

An Imprint of
SCHOLASTIC

New York Toronto London Auckland Sydney Mexico City New Delhi Hong Kong

ISBN 978-0-545-14095-9

ISBN 978-0-545-14096-6 (paperback)

ACKNOWLEDGMENTS

Cover and interior artwork by Jeff Smith

Text by Jeff Smith and Tom Sniegoski

Harvestar Family Crest designed by Charles Vess

Map of *The Valley* by Mark Crilley

Color by Steve Hamaker

10 9 8 7 6 5 4 3 2 1 10 11 12 13

First Scholastic edition, August 2010

Book design by David Saylor

Printed in the United States 113

I dedicate this book to the memory of Gran'ma Smith,
who used to tell me some whoppers. – J.S.

For Jeff and Vijaya . . . Thanks so much for
sharing your toys with me. – T.S.

CONTENTS

SMILEY AND THE BONE SCOUTS

BONE

WHAT DO YOU **THINK**, BARTLEBY?

I THINK IT'S **PERFECT**!

ME, **TOO**!

C'MON OUT, BONE SCOUTS! WE'RE MAKIN' CAMP RIGHT HERE!

OH, **BOY**!

FIRST THINGS FIRST! SINCE I'M THE LEADER, IT'S TIME FOR ME TO PUT ON THE **BIG HAT!**

ALL RIGHT, SCOUTS!
ROLL CALL!

RINGO!
BINGO!
TODD!
BARTLEBY!
SMILEY!

ALL PRESENT AND ACCOUNTED FOR, CAPTAIN!
GOOD!

OKAY, TEAM, LET'S GET TO WORK. WE'LL PUT OUR TENTS OVER THERE - -
OVER **THERE?**

THAT'S A TERRIBLE PLACE FOR OUR TENTS.
WHO'S WEARING THE BIG HAT, TODD?

BUT LOOK AT IT!
TUT! TUT! THE HAT HAS SPOKEN!

IS THIS THE SAME HAT THAT DECIDED TO WAIT UNTIL DARK TO SET UP OUR TENTS?
C'MON, I'LL HELP CLEAR OUT THE ROCKS!
THERE YOU GO, TEAMWORK. IT BUILDS CHARACTER, TODD.

RINGO AND BINGO, YOU SET UP THE TENTS . . .
TODD, YOU GET STARTED ON THE CAMPFIRE.
YES, SIR.

MEANWHILE, I'LL UNPACK THE RATIONS!
A LOAF OF BREAD...
A JAR OF PEANUT BUTTER...

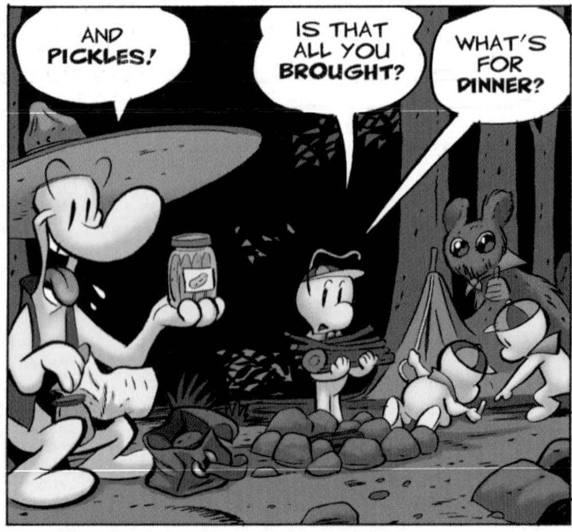
AND PICKLES!
IS THAT ALL YOU BROUGHT?
WHAT'S FOR DINNER?

PEANUT BUTTER & PICKLE SANDWICHES!
EW!
YEEE!

SEE? THAT'S WHY YOU GUYS AREN'T WEARING THE BIG HAT. IT TAKES BIG IDEAS TO WEAR THIS BABY!
OH MY GOSH! I THINK HE'S ACTUALLY GONNA EAT IT!

MM! CRUNCH! SMUNCH CRUNCH!
AAHG!
YUCK!
THE BIG HAT IS TRYING TO KILL US!

DON'T WORRY, GUYS -- I BROUGHT HOT DOGS!
HOORAY!

ALL RIGHT, BUT YOU'RE MISSING OUT ON A TASTY TREAT!
HOT DOGS OVER A CAMPFIRE -- NOW **THAT'S** A TASTY TREAT!
YEAH!
TELL US A STORY, SMILEY!

A STORY?
YEAH, TELL US ABOUT THE **VALLEY!**

WE WANT TO HEAR THE ADVENTURES OF YOU AND YOUR COUSINS AFTER YOU GOT **LOST** IN THE MYSTERIOUS VALLEY **FAR, FAR AWAY!**

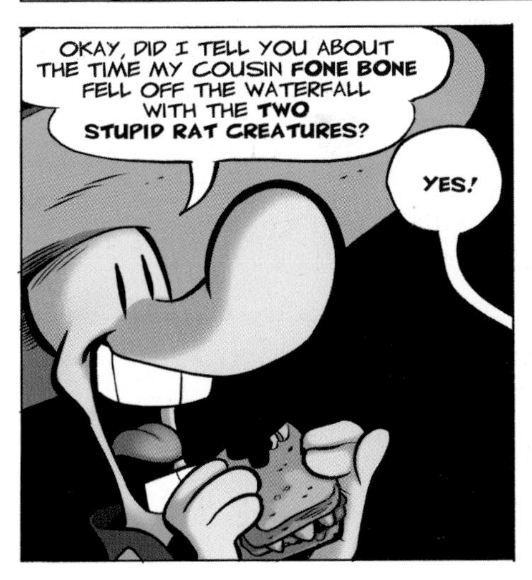
OKAY, DID I TELL YOU ABOUT THE TIME MY COUSIN **FONE BONE** FELL OFF THE WATERFALL WITH THE **TWO STUPID RAT CREATURES?**
YES!

LET'S SEE . . . DID I TELL YOU ABOUT **THE GREAT COW RACE?** OR ABOUT THE TIME WE MET **ROCK JAW,** THE GIANT **MOUNTAIN LION?**
YES!
AND **YES!**

Oh-- WAIT!
HOW ABOUT THE TIME THORN TRIED TO GET FONE BONE AND PHONEY BONE TO DO LAUNDRY?
LAUNDRY? WE WANT AN ADVENTURE!
THORN? YOU MEAN QUEEN THORN?

SHE WASN'T QUEEN YET! THIS WAS WHILE WE WERE STILL LIVING ON GRAN'MA BEN'S FARM.

OKAY, SO. . . ME AND FONE, WE LIKED LIVIN' ON THE FARM, BUT OUR RICH COUSIN PHONEY WAS HAVING A HARD TIME.

PHONEY DOESN'T REALLY BELIEVE IN WORK, AND WE ALL USED TO TAKE TURNS DOING THE CHORES.
WELL, ONE DAY, WHILE I WAS BUSY WORKING ON THE FARMHOUSE ROOF. . .

BONE
FONE BONE! PHONEY BONE! IT'S YOUR DAY TO DO THE LAUNDRY!
DON'T WORRY, THORN! WE DIDN'T FORGET!
NOT US! WE'LL GET RIGHT ON IT!
YOU EVER NOTICE HOW SIMPLE AN' UNCOMPLICATED EVERYTHING IS HERE? KINDA MAKES YOU REALIZE WHAT TH' REALLY IMPORTANT THINGS IN LIFE ARE!
LIKE SHOVELIN' OUT COW BARNS? YOU CAN KEEP IT! I MISS TH' HUSTLE AN' BUSTLE OF GOOD OL' BONEVILLE!
YOU MISS WORRYING ABOUT YOUR MONEY! WELL, THERE ISN'T ANY MONEY HERE, SO WHY NOT RELAX AN' RESIGN YOURSELF TO FATE?
FATE?! DON'T MAKE ME LAUGH! THERE'S PLENTY OF FORCES AROUND MORE POWERFUL THAN FATE!

HELLO!
WHAT'S THIS?

IT'S A TREASURE MAP! SO MUCH FOR YOUR CUTESY, LITTLE POWERS OF FATE!

WE WERE LED TO THIS MAP BY THE ULTIMATE PROVIDENCE! THIS, MY FRIEND, IS TH' WORKINGS OF CAPITALISM!

TH' ULTIMATE PROVIDENCE?
IT LOOKS LIKE TH' TREASURE IS BURIED UNDER A TREE SHAPED LIKE TH' LETTER N! C'MON! LET'S FOLLOW THIS THING!

WE CAN'T FOLLOW IT THAT WAY! IT GOES STRAIGHT DOWN THROUGH A BRIAR PATCH!
I'M NOT GONNA GIVE UP THAT EASY! WITH THIS TREASURE WE CAN RETURN TO BONEVILLE IN TRIUMPH! C'MON! WE'LL GO AROUND!

NO AMOUNT OF TREASURE IS WORTH THIS!
JUST A LITTLE FARTHER! I THINK THERE'S A PATH!

I DON'T KNOW. IT DOESN'T LOOK TOO SAFE - - -
CRACK

SHOOMP!

MAN! IF THIS GIANT NEST HADN'T BEEN HERE WE WOULDA BEEN KILLED! TELL ME YOU DON'T BELIEVE IN FATE NOW!
FATE, SHMATE! LET'S JUST HOPE TH' PARENT DOESN'T COME BACK!

DON'T PANIC.
DON'T MAKE ANY
SUDDEN MOVES . . .

GULP!
WHOA!

LEGGO,
YA BIG
BUZZARD!

SPIT 'IM OUT
OR I START
CHUCKIN' EGGS
OVER TH'
SIDE!

PT-OO!

JUMP!

WHEE-HAW!
OW! OW! OW! OW!

LOOK!

THE LETTER N!

OH MY GOSH! IT'S REAL!
WHAT DO WE DO NOW?
OKAY! OKAY! THERE'S TEN LITTLE FOOTPRINTS LEADING TO TH' WEST OF TH' TREE . . .

1, 2, 3, 4, 5 . . .

6, 7, 8, 9...

10!

HERE IT IS! I KNEW MY FAITH IN TH' POWER OF CAPITALISM WOULD MAKE ME RICH!
HERE'S A SHOVEL!

THIS IS MY LUCKY DAY! THANK YOU, O POWERS THAT BE!
DO YOU HONESTLY BELIEVE THAT CAPITALISM IS A POWER THAT BE?!

I'M TELLIN' YA, FONE BONE! IT'S A COSMIC FORCE IN ITS OWN RIGHT!
HEY! I HIT SOMETHIN'!

QUICK! OPEN IT UP! WHAT IS IT? GOLD? CROWN JEWELS? WHAT? WHAT?!
IT'S A BUNCH OF DIRTY CLOTHES.

WHAT?
IN FACT, IT'S YOUR DIRTY CLOTHES!

DO YOU THINK THORN IS TRYING TO TELL US SOMETHING?
EITHER THAT, OR TH' POWERS THAT BE WANT US TO DO OUR LAUNDRY!

...AND THAT WAS THE LAST TIME FONE BONE AN' PHONEY TRIED TO GET OUT OF LAUNDRY DUTY!
NO WAY!
WHAT A GREAT STORY!
IS IT TRUE?

OF COURSE IT'S TRUE, TODD! I'VE GOT THE BIG HAT ON!
TELL US ANOTHER STORY, SMILEY!

OKAY, WHAT ABOUT?
TELL US A STORY ABOUT BONEVILLE!

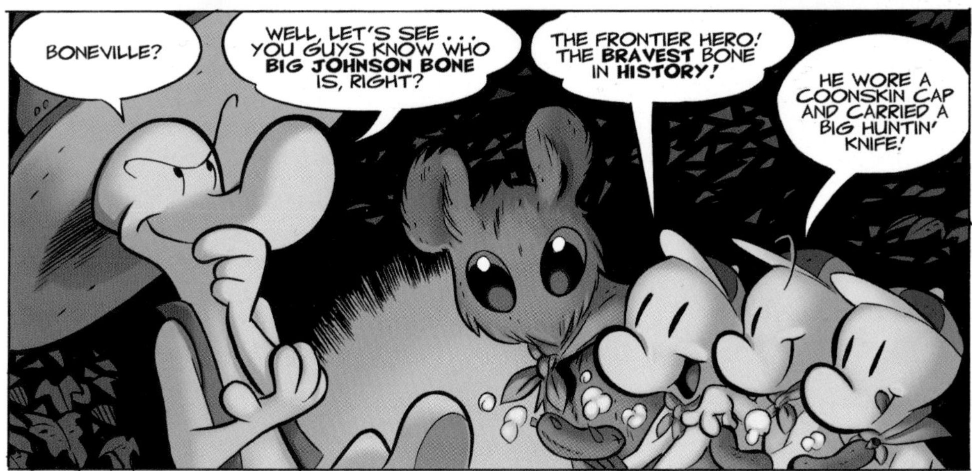
BONEVILLE?
WELL, LET'S SEE . . . YOU GUYS KNOW WHO BIG JOHNSON BONE IS, RIGHT?
THE FRONTIER HERO! THE BRAVEST BONE IN HISTORY!
HE WORE A COONSKIN CAP AND CARRIED A BIG HUNTIN' KNIFE!

THAT'S RIGHT! HE WAS TH' ROUGHEST, TOUGHEST BONE THAT EVER LIVED!
BUT DID YOU KNOW THAT BIG JOHNSON BONE WAS THE FOUNDER OF BONEVILLE?

THERE'S A STATUE OF HIM IN FRONT OF CITY HALL BECAUSE HE BUILT THE FIRST TRADING POST ON THE ROLLING BONE RIVER!

BUT BEFORE ALL THAT, HE WAS JUST A LITTLE, BITTY BABY, BORN IN A LOG CABIN . . .

. . . AND HE ALMOST DIDN'T LIVE THROUGH HIS FIRST DAY!
REALLY?
TELL US!

IT ALL HAPPENED IN THE MIDDLE OF WINTER . . .

BABY JOHNSON
BONE
VS.
OLD MAN WINTER
IT WAS ESPECIALLY COLD THAT YEAR, AS IF THE SEASON OF ICE AND SNOW WAS TRYING TO TEACH THE SETTLERS A LESSON.
WINTER WAS THE MEANEST OF THE SEASONS, READY TO TAKE YOU IN ITS ICY GRIP AND YANK THE WARMTH RIGHT OUT OF YOUR BONES JUST TO PROVE HOW TOUGH IT WAS.
YEP, WINTER WAS TOUGH, BUT SOMETHING SPECIAL WAS ABOUT TO COME ALONG THAT WAS EVEN TOUGHER.
STRANGE THING WAS, WINTER SEEMED TO SENSE A CHALLENGE COMIN', AND DIDN'T CARE ONE LITTLE BIT.

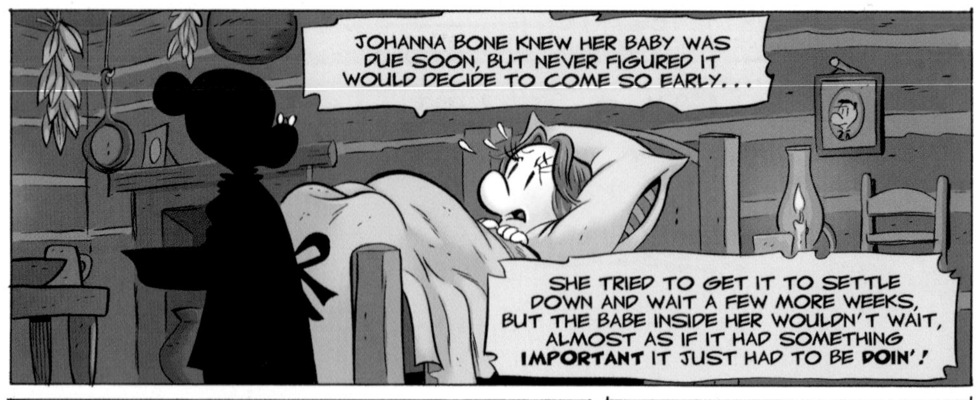
JOHANNA BONE KNEW HER BABY WAS DUE SOON, BUT NEVER FIGURED IT WOULD DECIDE TO COME SO EARLY...
SHE TRIED TO GET IT TO SETTLE DOWN AND WAIT A FEW MORE WEEKS, BUT THE BABE INSIDE HER WOULDN'T WAIT, ALMOST AS IF IT HAD SOMETHING **IMPORTANT** IT JUST HAD TO BE **DOIN'**!

IT WAS PURE LUCK THAT BROUGHT OLD HEPZIBAH BONE TO THE CABIN THAT NASTY WINTER'S DAY, NEEDIN' **TUBERS** FOR A POT OF STEW.
THAT'S IT, GIRL, YOU'RE DOIN' FINE. GOOD THING I HAD ME A HANKERIN' FOR **TUBER STEW** OR YOU'D BE DOIN' THIS BY YER **LONESOME!**

BY HER LONESOME IS HOW JOHANNA LIVED EVER SINCE HER HUSBAND, JEBIDIAH BONE, HAD GONE OFF HUNTING LATE LAST WINTER AN' NEVER FOUND HIS WAY BACK...
UNGH! STEW... SOUNDS PRETTY GOOD RIGHT ABOUT NOW. **ARRGH!** ...JEBIDIAH ALWAYS LIKED HIS STEW.

JOHANNA'S BABY WAS COMING, AND OUTSIDE THE STORM **HOWLED**, AS IF WARNING THE YOUNGIN ON THE WAY THAT LIFE WASN'T **EASY**, THAT THINGS WERE **TOUGH** OUT IN THE WILDERNESS, AND A CERTAIN AMOUNT OF **RESPECT** NEEDED TO BE SHOWN TO TH' **ELEMENTS**.
WWOOOOOOOOOOOO

ESPECIALLY TO **WINTER**.

OOOOOOWW
LISTEN TO THAT **WIND**. YOU'D THINK THERE WAS A PACK OF **WOLVES** JUST OUTSIDE THE DOOR... TRYIN' TO GET **IN!**

BANG
SOUNDS TO ME LIKE WINTER'S GOT A LOT TO SAY ABOUT THIS CHILD . . . THIS ONE MIGHT BE SPECIAL.
HE'S COMIN'!
BAM!

HE'S HERE!
WAAH!

WHOA!
SLOW DOWN, YOUNG FELLER!
WHY, HE'S JUST FULL OF FIGHT! AN' GOOD LUNGS, TOO!
WAUGH!
THAT'S NOT JUST ANY BONE, HEPZIBAH, THAT'S JOHNSON BONE . . .
. . . MY SON!

BANG!
CLAP!
BANG
LEMME JES' CLEAN THE LITTLE TYKE UP . . .

BAM!

SAY HOWDY-DO TO YOUR --
Oh!
WHEEE!

THE WINTER SNATCHED THE YOUNG BONE AWAY BEFORE IT COULD EVEN KNOW THE GENTLE TOUCH OF ITS MOTHER.

THE WIND IS CARRYING HIM OVER THE MOUNTAINS!

HE'S GONE.
JOHANNA, HONEY, YOU'RE TOO WEAK... YOU GOT TO GO BACK WHERE IT'S WARM. I'LL GO AFTER THE TYKE!

NO, WAIT!
I NEED A TUBER!
A TUBER? WHATEVER FOR?!

POOR THING! SHE'S TOUCHED IN THE HEAD. I'LL HAVE TO FIND THE BABY MYSELF!

JUST AS WINTER HAD TAKEN JOHANNA'S HUSBAND, IT NOW CLAIMED HER SON AS WELL. BUT SOMETHING TOLD HER IT WOULD NOT BE ABLE TO KEEP HIM. HER BOY WAS A FIGHTER.

PLOP!

!

HA! HA! HA!

HELLO, BABY JOHNSON BONE! I AM OLD MAN WINTER!

YOU DON'T LOOK SO SPECIAL OR TOUGH TO ME!

I'M WINTER! TH' TOUGHEST SEASON OF ALL, AN' NOBODY CAN--

BONK!

BRAT!

LET'S SEE HOW SPECIAL YOU ARE AGAINST AN ANGRY CAVE BEAR!

RRRRRRRR

BONK!

ROAR!

HA! HA! HA!

NOBODY CAN CHALLENGE MY POWER!

WHAT?!!
PAT
PAT
PAT

MEANWHILE, HEPZIBAH WAS ABOUT TO GIVE UP HOPE . . .
I'LL NEVER FIND THE LITTLE TYKE IN THIS STORM. IF ONLY THE BLIZZARD WOULD LET UP - -

THEN, A MIRACLE OCCURRED!
GLORY BE! THE WIND AND THE SNOW JUST STOPPED!
AN TH' SUN IS COMIN' OUT!

SNIFF! SNIFF!
SAKES ALIVE! IT'S BABY JOHNSON BONE!

SON! WHERE YOU GOIN'?
I SWAN! APPEARS HE'S ON TH' SCENT OF SOME CRITTER!
SNIFF!
SNIFF! SNIFF!

WHY, HE AIN'T AFTER NO CRITTER - - HE'S ON THE SCENT OF HIS OWN MA'S TUBER STEW!

I KNEW MY BOY COULDN'T RESIST TH' PLEASING AROMA OF MY HEARTY STEW!
COME AN' GET IT!

AIN'T YOU A SIGHT! WE HAVEN'T BEEN PROPERLY INTRODUCED, BUT I'M YOUR MOMMA!
MA!
JOHANNA HAD A FEELING THIS BABY WAS SPECIAL . . .

AND I AM SO VERY PLEASED TO MAKE YOUR ACQUAINTANCE, JOHNSON BONE!
OL' MA!
SHE KNEW IF ANYONE COULD TEACH OLD MAN WINTER A LESSON, IT WAS HER LITTLE BABY JOHNSON BONE!

. . . AND THAT, MY LITTLE FRIENDS, IS WHY WE HAVE SPRING!
NO KIDDIN'?
THAT'S SO COOL!
OH, COME ON!

BE QUIET, TODD!
SAY, WHY DOESN'T BARTLEBY TELL US A STORY?

ME? BUT RAT CREATURES AREN'T VERY GOOD AT TELLING STORIES.
WHAT WOULD I TELL?

YOU ONCE TOLD ME ABOUT A MONSTER THAT ALL RAT CREATURES ARE AFRAID OF!
YOU MEAN THE JEKK? IT'S BECAUSE OF THE JEKK THAT RAT CREATURES DON'T HAVE TAILS!

YES! TELL US WHY RAT CREATURES DON'T HAVE TAILS!
IT'S REALLY ONLY A LEGEND. I'M SURE . . .
TELL US!
FINALLY! A REAL STORY!

WELL, WHEN WE'RE BORN, WE HAVE LONG, BEAUTIFUL, HAIRLESS TAILS, BUT ON OUR FIRST BIRTHDAY, WE HAVE TO GET THEM CUT OFF.
THAT'S AMAZING! RAT CREATURES ACTUALLY HAVE TAILS, AND YOU CUT 'EM OFF - - ?
WHY?!

BECAUSE IF WE DON'T, THE JEKK WILL COME IN THE MIDDLE OF THE NIGHT AND DRAG US AWAY BY OUR TAILS.
THE END!
THE END?
WAIT. . . . THAT'S IT?

YEAH, SORRY. I TOLD YOU RAT CREATURES AREN'T VERY GOOD AT TELLING STORIES.

MAYBE YOU SHOULD TELL US ANOTHER STORY, SMILEY!
YES, PLEASE!
ONE MORE!

OKAY, TIME FOR ONE MORE. THIS STORY IS ABOUT BIG JOHNSON BONE VERSUS . . .

. . . THE COBBLER GOBBLER!!

BIG JOHNSON BONE VS. THE COBBLER GOBBLER
IT WAS THE LATE SUMMER OF HIS FIFTEENTH YEAR, AND BIG JOHNSON BONE HAD AWAKENED BRIGHT AND EARLY ON THAT BIG DAY, UNAWARES OF JUST HOW BIG IT WAS GOING TO BE.
IT WAS THE FIRST DAY OF THE BONE COUNTY FESTIVAL, THE DAY ON WHICH THE TERRITORIES' BIGGEST EATING COMPETITION WAS HELD.
I'VE GOT ANOTHER FULL BATCH OF FLAPJACKS ON THE GRIDDLE, THREE POUNDS OF BACON WAITIN' TO BE FIXED, AND A TURKEY THAT SHOULD BE JUST ABOUT DONE.
THINK I'M GONNA PUT A CORK IN IT FOR RIGHT NOW, MA.

BUT YOU'VE BARELY EATEN A THING!
HOW YOU GONNA BEAT ALL THEM OTHER HUNGRY BOYS FROM THE TERRITORIES IF YOU DON'T STRETCH OUT THEM BELLY MUSCLES?

DON'T WORRY ABOUT MY BELLY. I LIKE TO TEASE IT A BIT BEFORE THE REAL CHOW TIME BEGINS. DON'T I, BUDDY?
SMURGLE
GURGLE
WELL, SIR, BEST GET A MOVE ON.

HAVE A GOOD TIME, SON! AND TRY NOT TO EMBARRASS THEM POOR BOYS TOO MUCH NOW! I'LL HAVE LUNCH A-WAITIN' WHEN YOU GET BACK!
THANKS, MA! SEE YA LATER WITH MY NEW BLUE RIBBON!
BIG JOHNSON HAD WON THE GORGE-A-THON FOURTEEN YEARS IN A ROW, A STREAK HE HAD EVERY INTENTION OF CONTINUING.

MORNIN', FOLKS! ON YOUR WAY TO THE FAIR?
TO WATCH YOU, BIG JOHNSON! YOU GONNA EAT YOUR WEIGHT IN SAUSAGES TODAY?
HOW MANY FRUIT COBBLERS YOU GONNA GET DOWN TODAY, BIG JOHNSON?
MY DADDY SAYS NOBODY CAN EAT AS MUCH AS YOU, BIG JOHNSON!

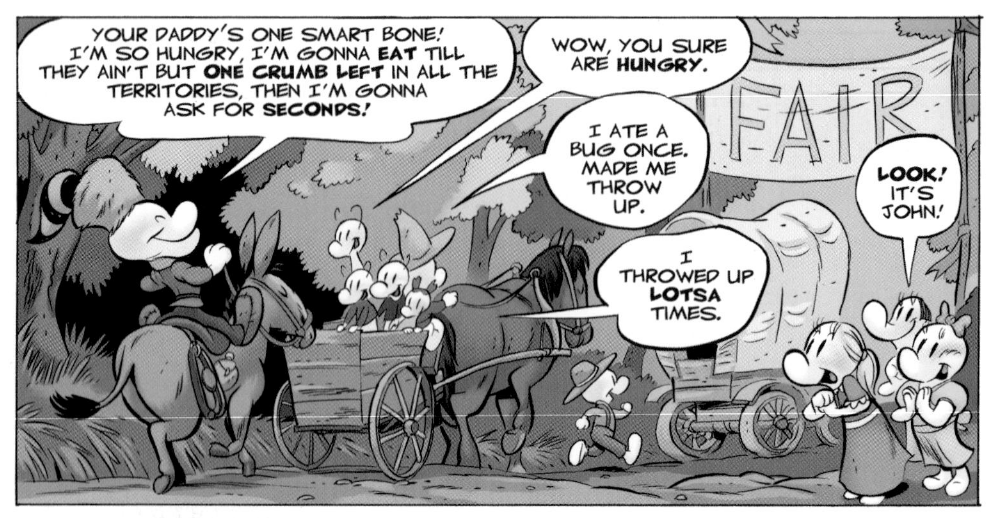
YOUR DADDY'S ONE SMART BONE! I'M SO HUNGRY, I'M GONNA EAT TILL THEY AIN'T BUT ONE CRUMB LEFT IN ALL THE TERRITORIES, THEN I'M GONNA ASK FOR SECONDS!
WOW, YOU SURE ARE HUNGRY.
I ATE A BUG ONCE. MADE ME THROW UP.
I THROWED UP LOTSA TIMES.
FAIR
LOOK! IT'S JOHN!

LADIES.
HELLO, JOHN.
GONNA WIN TODAY, JOHN?

'COURSE HE'S GONNA WIN! HOW COULD YOU ASK SUCH A THING . . . RIGHT, JOHN?

THERE THEY GO AGAIN, GUSHIN' ALL OVER HIM AND CARRYING ON LIKE HE'S OH SO SPECIAL!
FAIR
TO THE FAIR

LET'S SEE WHO THEY'RE GUSHIN' OVER ONCE THIS GORGE-A-THON IS DONE. WE'LL SEE HOW HIGH AND MIGHTY MR. BIG JOHNSON BONE IS WHEN I'M WEARIN THAT BLUE RIBBON.

YOU? DON'T KID YOURSELF! I PURPOSELY WORE ALL SHADES A BLUE TODAY SO'S THE RIBBON WOULD MATCH MY ENSEMBLE!
YEP, JOHNSON BONE IS GOIN' HOME IN TEARS THIS YEAR!
!
TO THE FAIR

BIG JOHN! THERE YOU ARE, M'BOY! THE PRIDE OF BONE COUNTY!
COME! COME! IT'S TIME TO GET STARTED!
BLOW THE HORN, ALGERNON!
SNIIIIFF! AHH! I CAN SMELL TH' RIBS COOKIN' FROM HERE, MR. MAYOR!

BRAAAPPP
ATTENTION, EVERYONE! TAKE YOUR POSITIONS, WE'RE COMMENCIN' TO START THE GORGE-A-THON!
'SCUSE ME, LADIES, BUT I GOT A EATIN' CONTEST TO WIN!

I HEAR YOU GOT SOME COMPETITION THIS YEAR, JOHN, BUT YOU KIN HANDLE IT, RIGHT? WE'RE ALL COUNTIN' ON YOU!
NOTHING WRONG WITH A LITTLE COMPETITION, MAYOR, JUST AS LONG AS THEY KNOW THEY CAN'T WIN - - NO HOW, NO WAY!

WELL, THAT'S NOT WHAT SHE SAYS . . .
SHE?

YES, SHE!! NAME'S GERTIE, BUT EVERYONE CALLS ME THE COBBLER GOBBLER ON ACCOUNT OF MY VORACIOUS ABILITY TO CONSUME VAST AMOUNTS OF FRUIT COBBLER - -
- - AS WELL AS OTHER FOOD-TYPE ITEMS!
GORGE-A-TH
SO YOU'RE BIG JOHNSON BONE! I HEAR YOU'RE SUPPOSED TO GIVE ME SOME COMPETITION . . .

. . . BUT IT MUST BE SOME OTHER BIG JOHNSON BONE, CAUSE YOU AIN'T ALL THAT!
I'M GONNA KICK YER PATOOTIE!

HAW!
UH, OH!

SHE'S WONDERFUL.
SHE'S YOUR **COMPETITION!** GERTIE'S FROM THE NEXT COUNTY **OVER!**

NOW GET UP ON THAT PLATFORM, AN' MAKE US **PROUD!**
BLOW TH' HORN, ALGERNON.

BRAAAP
PLACES, FOLKS! TIME FOR THE GORGE-A-THON'S FIRST ROUND! BRING OUT . . .
THE RIBS!
GORGE-A-THON

BRRAPPPP
GO!
GOB!
GLUB!
SLURP!
GARF!

THE SOUND OF THE STARTING HORN BROKE HIM FROM HIS STUPOR, AND BIG JOHNSON REMEMBERED WHY HE WAS THERE . . .
NO MATTER HOW BEAUTEOUS ONE OF HIS OPPONENTS WAS, HE HAD A RIBBON TO TAKE HOME. IT WAS A MATTER OF **PRIDE!**

SLOBBER
SLOB
CHEW
CHEW

GLOMPF
GLOBBER
SLURRP!
SMEK!
SMEK!
SMEK!

ROUND TWO . . .
GIANT SANDWICHES!
GOP!
GUP!
SMACK!

GOBBLE
SNARF!
ROMF

GULP
CHOMP
MP
CHOMP
SNAP

ROLMF
CHEW!

MUMF MUMF PTLAGH
GULP!
GRAWMF!
CHOMP GOB!
ROUND THREE . . . ASPARAGUS PIES!
ROUND FOUR . . . FRUIT COBBLER!
BITE!
SQUISH!
THAT'S ALL! I QUIT!
ME, TOO!
I'M OUT!
PLOP
GO ON, JOHN! SWALLOW THAT LAST BITE, AND YOU WIN!
HUH?

WHAT ARE YOU WAITING FOR?

SHOVE
GOB GUB GUB BLUB

GULP!

GERTIE WINS?
GERTIE WINS!!
SMURGLE
WHOOPS--
RRRRRG

HURRAY!
HUR
SHOOT.

LAND SAKES, MISS GERTIE, YOU'RE BLOWIN' UP SOMETHIN' FIERCE --
IT'S JUST A LITTLE GAS.
BLURRBLE
I'M SURE IT'LL PASS --

BRAAAAPPP

WHAT TH' HECK HAPPENED?
HOO-DAWGGIES! WHAT A WOMAN!
WHERE'S THE PLATFORM?

IT'S GONE - -
HEY - - WHERE'S GERTIE?

LOOK!

THAT WAS THE LAST TIME BIG JOHNSON EVER SAW HIS BELOVED COBBLER GOBBLER.
GERTIE HAD SET A NEW WORLD RECORD FOR ASPARAGUS PIES AND PEACH COBBLER, AND SHE BLEW HERSELF AND THE PLATFORM TO THE MOON.
THEY SAY SHE'S THERE STILL.

AFTER THAT, BIG JOHNSON WAS SO DEPRESSED THAT HE WANDERED IN THE WILDERNESS FOR THE NEXT TEN YEARS.
THEY SAY HE HAD **WONDROUS ADVENTURES**!
TELL US ABOUT THEM!

I CAN'T. IT'S A **MYSTERY**! NO ONE KNOWS WHERE HE **WENT**, OR WHAT HE **DID** - - UNTIL HE SETTLED DOWN ON THE ROLLING BONE RIVER AND STARTED UP HIS FAMOUS TRADING POST!

WOW. WHAT DO YOU THINK OF **THAT** STORY, TODD?
I'M SPEECHLESS.

WELL, WE BETTER CALL IT A NIGHT. WE HAVE A BIG HIKE TOMORROW!
AW!

LET'S PUT OUT THE FIRE AND GET READY FOR BED.
DONE!
CHECK!

GOOD NIGHT, RINGO, BINGO, AND TODD!
GOOD NIGHT, SMILEY!
GOOD NIGHT, BARTLEBY!

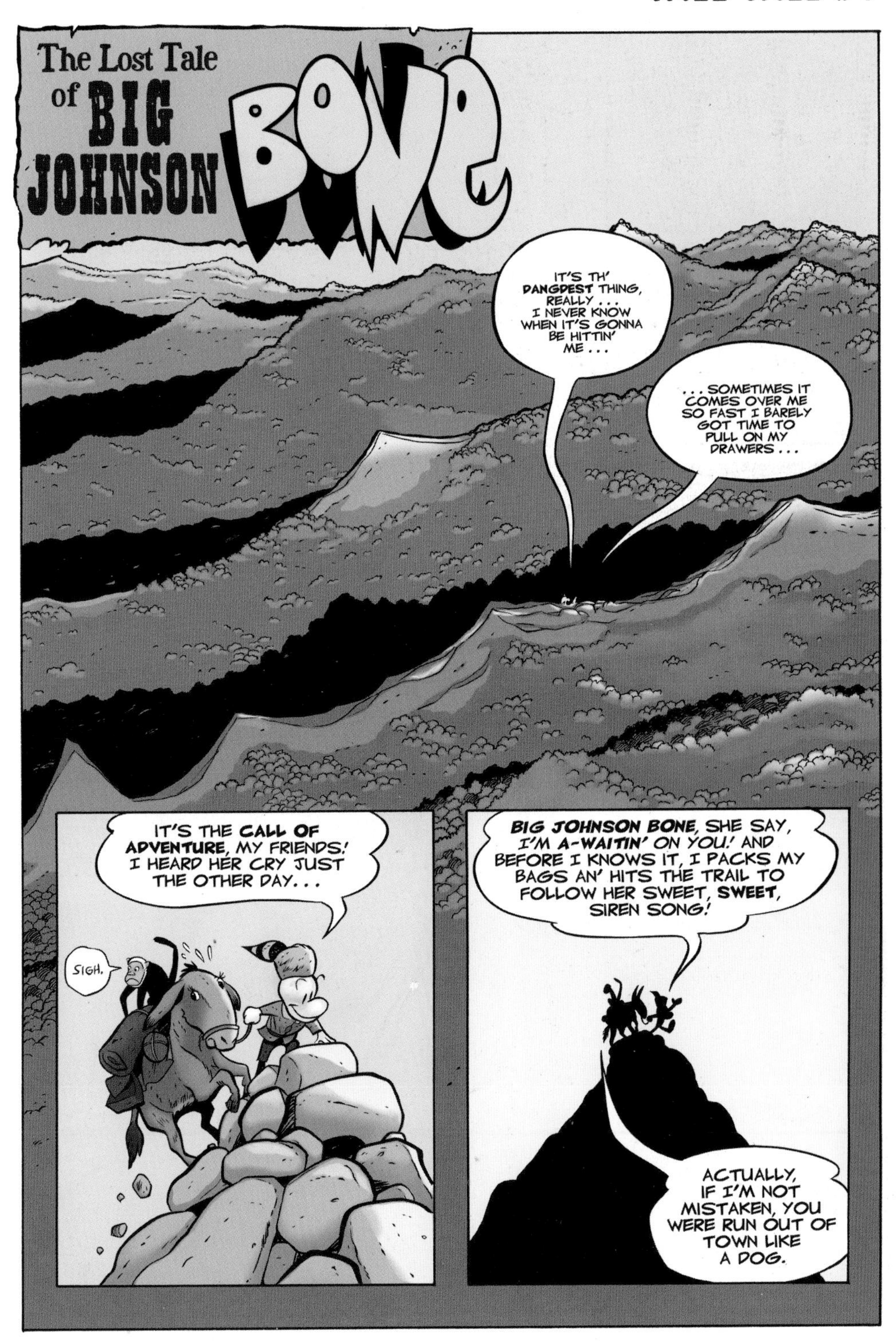
The Lost Tale of BIG JOHNSON BONE
IT'S TH' DANGDEST THING, REALLY . . . I NEVER KNOW WHEN IT'S GONNA BE HITTIN' ME . . .
. . . SOMETIMES IT COMES OVER ME SO FAST I BARELY GOT TIME TO PULL ON MY DRAWERS . . .
IT'S THE CALL OF ADVENTURE, MY FRIENDS! I HEARD HER CRY JUST THE OTHER DAY. . .
SIGH.
BIG JOHNSON BONE, SHE SAY, I'M A-WAITIN' ON YOU! AND BEFORE I KNOWS IT, I PACKS MY BAGS AN' HITS THE TRAIL TO FOLLOW HER SWEET, SWEET, SIREN SONG!
ACTUALLY, IF I'M NOT MISTAKEN, YOU WERE RUN OUT OF TOWN LIKE A DOG.

WELL, WHO'DA THUNK THEY'D GET SO GOSH-DARNED FIRED UP OVER A GAME OF **CARDS?**
ALL'S I WON WAS A **MONKEY**, FOR CRYIN' OUT LOUD.
AHEM, YES, A MONKEY. LET ME AGAIN REMIND YOU THAT THIS MONKEY HAS A **NAME** -- *MR. PIP.* AND YOU **CHEATED!**

WON YOU FAIR AND SQUARE, MR. POOP--
IT'S PIP! **PIP!**
WHATEVER. LADY LUCK WAS LOOKIN' DOWN AN' BLESSED ME WITH A **WINNIN' HAND.** SIMPLE AS THAT.

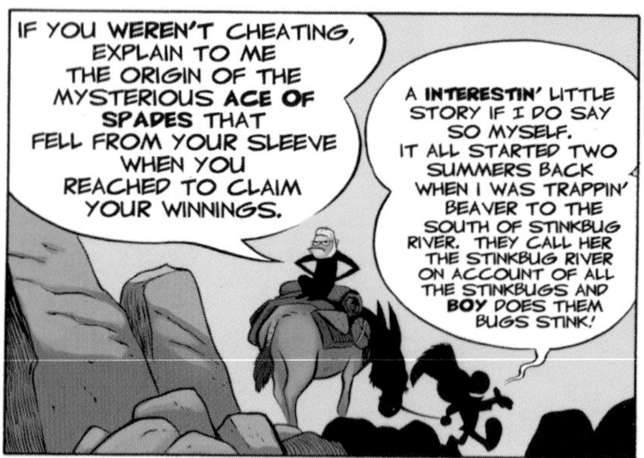
IF YOU **WEREN'T** CHEATING, EXPLAIN TO ME THE ORIGIN OF THE MYSTERIOUS **ACE OF SPADES** THAT FELL FROM YOUR SLEEVE WHEN YOU REACHED TO CLAIM YOUR WINNINGS.
A **INTERESTIN'** LITTLE STORY IF I DO SAY SO MYSELF. IT ALL STARTED TWO SUMMERS BACK WHEN I WAS TRAPPIN' BEAVER TO THE SOUTH OF STINKBUG RIVER. THEY CALL HER THE STINKBUG RIVER ON ACCOUNT OF ALL THE STINKBUGS AND **BOY** DOES THEM BUGS STINK!

--BUT BY THEN I'D ALREADY GONE TWO MONTHS WITHOUT A BITE TO EAT AND WAS FEELIN' A MITE CRANKY--

--AFTERWARDS, THEY DECLARED ME THE **WINNER**, BUT I KNEW TH' **JIG WAS UP!** SO I GRABBED TH' STUFFED POSSUM--

--THEN **WHAT DID I SEE** AT MY FEET? COMPLETELY UNTOUCHED BY THE EXPLOSION THAT LEVELED A GOOD HUNDRED MILES OF FOREST-- YES, **SIR**, THAT'S RIGHT, A SINGLE PLAYING CARD --AN **ACE OF SPADES** TO BE PRECISE.
SO I PICKED IT UP AND PUT IT INSIDE MY COAT IN CASE WHOEVER **LOST** IT CAME **LOOKIN'**.
DOES THAT ANSWER YOUR QUESTION?
Z

HUMPH! NO APPRECIATION FOR THE ART OF STORYTELLIN'. LAST TIME I WASTE A PERFECTLY GOOD YARN ON THE LIKES A **THEM!**

. . . AND THAT'S HOW WE LEARNED THAT ASPARAGUS CAN BE QUITE EXPLOSIVE TO THE MORE DELICATE DIGESTIVE SYSTEMS.

YET ANOTHER FASCINATING TALE.
DRAWING A MAP, ARE WE? HURRAH! I SUPPOSE THERE'S A CHANCE WE'LL BE ABLE TO FIND OUR WAY BACK, THEN.
DIDN'T KNOW MONKEYS WAS SO OVERFLOWIN' WITH ATTITUDE.
IF I'DA KNOWD I MIGHTA TAKEN YOUR FORMER OWNER'S BOOTS INSTEAD.

BESIDES, WE AIN'T EVER GOIN' BACK. I'M MAKIN' A MAP OF WHERE WE'RE GOIN' TO!
HOW CAN YOU MAKE A MAP OF SOMEWHERE YOU'VE NEVER BEEN?

SHOWS WHAT YOU KNOW ABOUT EXPLORING UNKNOWN TERRITORY.
JUST SO HAPPENS I'M ONE OF THE WORLD'S LEADIN' EXPLORERS, THANK YOU VERY MUCH.

CRUDONIA? SANDWICH LAND? VALLEY OF THE ALL-YOU-CAN-EAT BRATWURST CABBAGE BUFFET? DO ANY OF THESE RING A BELL, MR. PLOP?
I CANNOT BELIEVE A CRAZY PERSON NOW OWNS ME.

YOU A-DOUBTIN' MY WORD?!! BIG JOHNSON DON'T LIE!!! IF I'M A-LYIN', MAY A BIG OL' TWISTER DROP DOWN AN' SUCK ME UP!!

PLINK
SAY. . . IS THAT HAIL?
BINK
PLINK
OH, I HATE IT WHEN THE POWERS THAT BE LISTEN TO ME . . .

IT'S GETTING DARK! DO THE POWERS THAT BE LISTEN TO YOU VERY OFTEN?
LET'S JUST SAY THAT IT MIGHT BE IN OUR BEST INTERESTS TO RUN LIKE HECK!

A TWISTER?! YOU COULDN'T USE A GENTLE SUMMER RAIN TO MAKE YOUR POINT?
HOLD ON TO YOUR TAILS--

-- THESE THINGS CAN BE MIGHTY MEAN!
LET ME GUESS, YOU'VE HAD EXPERIENCE WITH TWISTERS BEFORE?

THAT'S EXACTLY RIGHT, SO DON'T BE GIVIN' UP THE GHOST JUST YET, MR. PEEP. I KNOWS A THING OR TWO ABOUT THESE DEVILS!
I'M TOO YOUNG TO DIE!

JUST GOTTA . . .

SHOW 'EM WHO'S BOSS, THAT'S ALL!

GRAB A HOLD, PEEP! WE'RE RIDIN' THIS WAVE!
OH, MY.

READY? HERE WE GO!
YAH!
YAH!
HA! HA! HA!

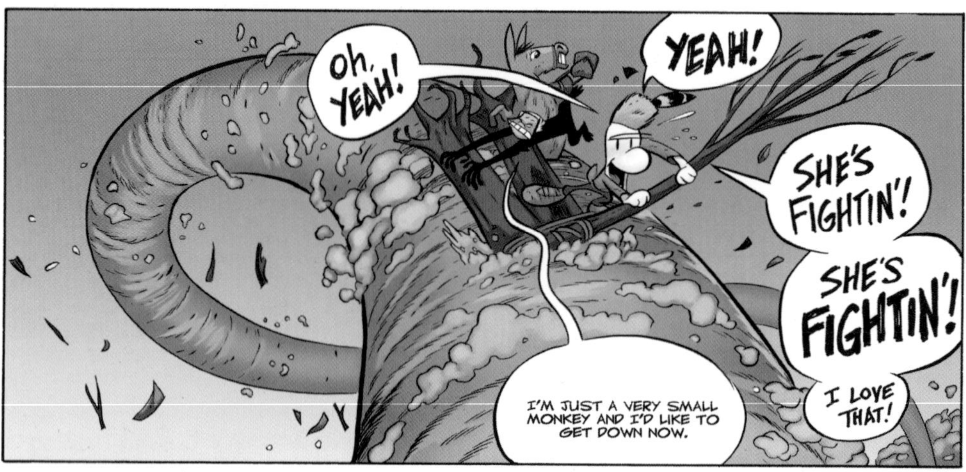
Oh, YEAH!
YEAH!
SHE'S FIGHTIN'!
SHE'S FIGHTIN'!
I LOVE THAT!
I'M JUST A VERY SMALL MONKEY AND I'D LIKE TO GET DOWN NOW.

YAH! GO ON! I WAS DONE WITH YA ANYWAY!
PLEASE . . . I DON'T WANT TO GO ROUND AND ROUND ANYMORE.

HA! HA! JUST LIKE OLD TIMES, EH, BLOSSOM, OL' GIRL?
NOW THAT'S ADVENTURE! YOU CAN SMELL IT IN THE AIR!
IS THAT WHAT I SMELL? I THOUGHT SOMETHING HAD GONE BAD.

NUTHIN' BAD ABOUT THAT SMELL, NO, SIR. GETS THE BLOOD PUMPIN'!
NOW, LET'S HAVE A LOOK AROUND AND SEE WHERE WE ARE.

LOTS OF ROCKS AN' BUSHES -- I THINK THAT'S A DINGLEBERRY BUSH OVER THERE.
MONSTERS!
NOPE, NO MONSTERS. BELIEVE ME, I KNOW A MONSTER WHEN I SEE ONE.

WHOOPS!
THERE'S ONE!
HISSS
MY HEART!

SKEE-DADDLE, BLOSSOM! THESE BOYS AIN'T HERE TO BE NEIGHBORLY!
BUT, MOMMY! I DON'T WANT TO JOIN THE CIRCUS.

SSSSS!
I WOULDN'T TURN AROUND UNLESS YOU'RE INTERESTED IN SCARIN' TEN YEARS OFF YER LIFE.
GIVEN UP AS A PRIZE IN A POKER GAME, SUCKED UP INTO A TWISTER, AND NOW CHASED BY MONSTERS - -

WHO DID I OFFEND TO DESERVE A FATE SUCH AS THIS?
CAN'T SAY IT'S BEEN BORIN'!

SSSS
Huff! Huff! Puff!

FASTER! RUN FASTER!
THIS REMINDS ME OF THE TIME I ACCIDENTALLY INTERRUPTED TH' SECRET MATING RITUALS OF SOME STRIPED WOOD PIXIES . . .

- - THEY DIDN'T HAVE NO BIG TEETH OR NASTY CLAWS - -

- - BUT BOY COULD THEY PINCH!

MM!
THE MAMMALS - - THEY GOT AWAY - - AND I WAS SO CLOSE!
THERE, THERE, COMRADE, NO NEED TO CONCERN YOURSELF . . .

ALL WE NEED TO DO IS GO BACK TO WHERE WE WERE RESTING AND WAIT FOR MORE MAMMALS TO FALL FROM THE SKY.
A MOST EXCELLENT IDEA, COMRADE. I COULD USE SOME REST AFTER ALL THE RUNNING I'VE JUST DONE.

CAN'T YOU RUN ANY FASTER? THEY'RE GAINING ON US!

WHAT ARE YOU DOING?!! GET UP! THE MONSTERS WILL BE HERE ANY MOMENT!
I THINK WE GAVE 'EM THE SLIP.

YOU'VE GOT TO GET US OUT OF HERE!
FIRST THING WE GOTTA DO IS FIGURE OUT WHERE THAT TWISTER DROPPED US.

WELL? WHAT DO YOU THINK? ARE WE IN BOLONEY LAND OR THE VALLEY OF THE BREAKING WINDS?
NOPE. AIN'T NONE OF THEM . . .

CAN'T SAY I HAVE THE FAINTEST **IDEA** WHERE WE ARE, MR. PEP. . .
BUT WHEREVER IT IS, IT SURE IS PURTY.

SNAP
RUSTLE!
RUSTLE!
THEY'VE FOUND US!
JOHNSON! YOU GET OVER HERE THIS INSTANT AND PROTECT US!

THERE! YOU SEE? WE'LL ALL BE DEAD IN A MINUTE IF YOU DON'T DO SOMETHING!
RUSTLE
SNAP!
DON'T GIT YER TAIL IN A BUNCH. I'M NOT DOIN' ANY MORE RUNNIN' FROM ANYBODY TODAY.

THAT'LL BE THE DAY- - BIG JOHNSON RUNS AWAY TWICE FROM ANY BEASTIE ON GOD'S GREEN EARTH.
NOW WHERE IS SHE? WHERE'S MY SPECIAL GIRL?

THERE YA ARE, DARLIN'!
I CALL HER PIECEMAKER! ON ACCOUNT OF THE CONDITION SHE LEAVES ANYTHING THAT TRIES TO MESS WITH US!
IF YOU CATCH MY DRIFT.

Y'GOTTA RESPECT NATURE, BUT SOMETIMES Y' GOTTA SHOW HER WHO'S BOSS.
THIS REMINDS ME OF THE TIME I WAS FORCED TO DO BATTLE WITH A CAVE BEAR - -
MAYBE BLOSSOM AND I SHOULD GET A HEAD START RUNNING IN CASE THIS GOES BAD?
- - IT WAS CLOSE FOR A WHILE, BUT I WHUPPED THE BEAR SO BAD HE GAVE ME ALL HIS TEETH JUST SO'S I WOULDN'T WHUP HIM NO MORE.

I'D RATHER HAVE A CAVE BEAR RIGHT NOW INSTEAD OF THOSE . . . THOSE . . . THINGS!

C'MON OUT, YA VARMINT! I'M BIG JOHNSON BONE - -AND THIS IS MY KNIFE!

WELL, ROLL ME IN DOUGH AND CALL ME FOR BREAKFAST - - YOU AIN'T MONSTERS.

BREAKFAST? I HAVEN'T HAD ANY BREAKFAST.
MOST IMPORTANT MEAL OF THE DAY.
MONSTERS? I HAVEN'T SEEN ANY MONSTERS.
I BET MONSTERS EAT BREAKFAST.
A MONSTER ATE MY UNCLE SIDNEY FOR BREAKFAST - - OR WAS IT LUNCH?
WHO ARE YOU?
DID YOU COME BECAUSE OF LILY'S WISH?

WELL, WELL, AIN'T YOU CUTE . . .
. . . IN A **TALKY** KINDA WAY.

YOU'RE TALL.
WHAT'S YOUR SHOE SIZE?
I LIKE GUM.
WHAT'S YOUR NAME?
NICE HAT.
YOU'RE NEW AROUND HERE.
I CAN'T BELIEVE IT! LILY'S WISH CAME TRUE.
I . . . I THINK MY HEAD'S ABOUT TO EXPLODE.

NOW HOLD IT, HOLD IT. . . ONE AT A **TIME**.
OKAY, UH . . . **YOU**.

WHO ARE YOU?

THE NAME'S **BONE**, BIG JOHNSON BONE, AND I'M THE **TOUGHEST**, **ROUGHEST**, **EXPLORINEST** EXPLORER **YOU'RE** LIKELY TO LAY YOUR BEADY LITTLE EYES ON.

HAVE YOU COME TO SAVE US . . . LIKE LILY WISHED FOR?
NOW WHAT IN THE WORLD COULD BE GOIN' ON IN SECH A BEAUTIFUL PLACE THAT YOU'D NEED **SAVIN'** FROM?
BESIDES ALL THE MONSTERS IN THE BUSHES AN' STUFF?

IT'S VERY COMPLICATED.
FOLLOW US!
STILLMAN WILL EXPLAIN EVERYTHING!
HE'S VERY SMART.
HE'S THE GUARDIAN OF THIS PART OF THE FOREST, Y'KNOW.

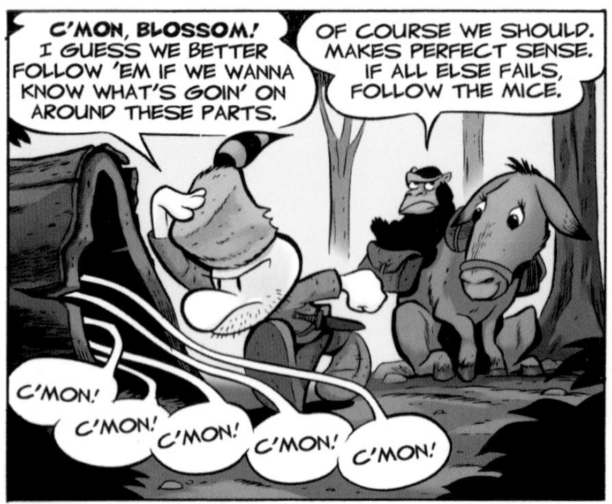
C'MON, BLOSSOM! I GUESS WE BETTER FOLLOW 'EM IF WE WANNA KNOW WHAT'S GOIN' ON AROUND THESE PARTS.
OF COURSE WE SHOULD. MAKES PERFECT SENSE. IF ALL ELSE FAILS, FOLLOW THE MICE.
C'MON!
C'MON!
C'MON!
C'MON!
C'MON!

HEY, YOU GUYS, IT'S US - - AND WE BROUGHT COMPANY!
HIS NAME IS BIG JOHNSON BONE!
I LIKE COMPANY.
I LIKE GUM.
HE'S AN EXPLORER!

A EXPLORER?
DID THEY COME TO HELP US?
THAT WOULD BE SWELL!
THAT'D BE AWESOME.

I'M LILY. ARE YOU MY WISH COME TRUE?
LILY MADE A WISH ON A FALLING STAR. I'M PETE.
I'M RAMONA AND THIS TURTLE IS PORTER. HE'S TOO AFRAID TO COME OUT OF HIS SHELL.
PLEASED TO MAKE YER ACQUAINTANCES. BUT I'M NOT HERE BECAUSE OF NO WISH. A TWISTER BRUNG ME.

DID YOU WISH FOR A TWISTER?
I DON'T THINK SO.
BUT HE'S HERE TO SAVE OUR FOLKS, RIGHT?
HERE, NOW! WHAT HAPPENED TO YER FOLKS THAT THEY NEED SAVIN'?

BANZAI!
POW!

WHAT IN TARNATION?

YOU!
GET OUT OF HERE, YOU - - YOU - - STRANGERS!
STILLMAN!
CEASE FIRE, STILLMAN.

THIS IS BIG JOHNSON BONE, AN' HE'S A EXPLORER.
HE'S OKAY, STILLMAN.
ARE YOU HURT?
NAH, NOT MUCH. GOT HIT IN THE HEAD BY THE MOON ONCE. NOW THAT HURT!

BIG JOHNSON BONE? WHAT KIND OF A NAME IS THAT? WHAT'S HE DOING IN OUR VALLEY?
RELAX, HE'S ONE OF THE GOOD GUYS.

BE NICE, STILLMAN. MR. BONE IS GOING TO HELP US SAVE OUR FOLKS!
HEY!
WE DON'T WANT HIM TO LEAVE!
YEAH, STILLMAN, BE NICE!
DON'T MIND ME FOR ASKING, BUT YOU'RE A DRAGON, AREN'T YOU?
YEAH, SO WHY YOU THROWIN' ROCKS, THEN? SHOULDN'T YOU BE BREATHIN' FIRE OR SOMETHIN' LIKE THAT?

HMMM. YES. BREATHING FIRE. RIGHT. **INTERESTING OBSERVATION.** I HAVE A PROBLEM, YOU SEE, WITH THE PROCESS OF BREATHING FLAME.

WHEN I **TRY** THERE'S THIS CONSTRICTION IN MY THROAT AND MY STOMACH GOES ALL **BLURPY** AND . . .
AND. . . ?

I GET VERY SICK.
THAT'S A REAL SHAME. ESPECIALLY BEIN' A DRAGON AND ALL.
THE CRITTERS HERE TELL ME YOU CAN EXPLAIN WHY THEIR FOLKS NEED TO BE SAVED.

IT'S THE **RAT CREATURES!** THEY'RE TRYING TO INCREASE THEIR TERRITORY!
ALL OF A SUDDEN THEY'RE **EVERYWHERE** AN' THEY'RE EATING **EVERYBODY!**

THE RAT CREATURES TOOK MY MOM AND DAD.
MINE, TOO.
THE RATS TOOK MY MOM AND DAD - - AND PORTER'S, TOO! HE HASN'T COME OUT OF HIS SHELL SINCE.
IT'S TRUE.

IT'S **MY** JOB TO **PROTECT** THE FOREST ANIMALS FROM THE RATS - -
I MEAN IT **USED** TO BE MY JOB - -
A MEMBER OF THE HIGH COUNCIL OF DRAGONS IS COMING HERE TO PICK A **NEW** PROTECTOR . . . I'M BEING **REPLACED.**

I GUESS THE HIGH COUNCIL OF DRAGONS MADE A MISTAKE WHEN THEY ASSIGNED A ROCK-THROWING DRAGON TO THIS NECK OF THE WOODS.
WE DON'T BLAME YOU, STILLMAN.
YES, WE KNOW YOU DID YOUR BEST.
NOBODY CAN STOP THE RAT CREATURES.

RAT CREATURES, HUH? I WONDER IF THEM'S THE SAME FOUL-SMELLIN' VARMINTS THAT CHASED ME AND MY CREW WHEN WE FIRST GOT HERE?
RAT CREATURES, YES, I **DO** BELIEVE THAT'S AN ADEQUATE MONIKER.

DID THEY HAVE REALLY, REALLY POINTY TEETH, LIKE **THIS?**

- - AND REALLY LONG **CLAWS?**

AND LONG, UGLY TAILS, NOT PRETTY LIKE MINE?

THAT'D BE THEM.
THIS ISN'T GOOD. THEY'RE COMING EVEN FARTHER INTO THE VALLEY NOW!

DON'T GET YER SCALES ALL BENT THE WRONG WAY, STILLMAN. LET ME PUFF MY PIPE AND THINK A SPELL - - I MIGHT JUST GET THE BEGINNING OF AN IDEA.
SOMEONE BE MERCIFUL AND END MY LIFE NOW.

IT'S NOT EASY BEING ME - - REALLY IT ISN'T.

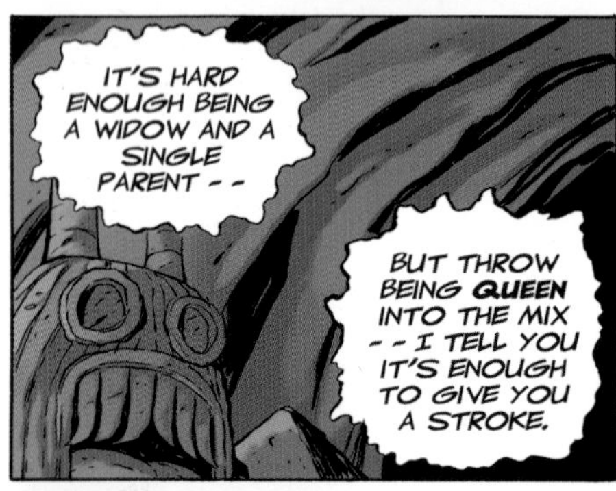
IT'S HARD ENOUGH BEING A WIDOW AND A SINGLE PARENT - -
BUT THROW BEING **QUEEN** INTO THE MIX - - I TELL YOU IT'S ENOUGH TO GIVE YOU A STROKE.

YOU JUST DON'T **KNOW** HOW MUCH I LOOK FORWARD TO THIS. WITH YOU I'M JUST ONE OF THE **GIRLS**, YOU KNOW?

YES, QUEEN MAUD. MAY I SAY YOUR TAIL IS LOOKING ESPECIALLY FETCHING TODAY.
WELL, YOU KNOW HOW I FEEL ABOUT A WELL-GROOMED TAIL. THE KING ALWAYS SAID, YOU CAN TELL A LOT ABOUT A RAT CREATURE BY THE CONDITION OF THEIR TAIL.'
BOY, I MISS HIM. WHO'DA THUNK THAT A BAD PIECE OF PORK COULD BE SO **DEVASTATING**?

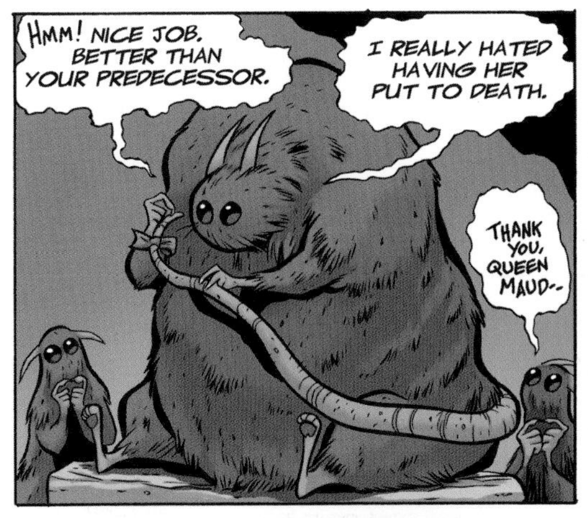
HMM! NICE JOB. BETTER THAN YOUR PREDECESSOR.
I REALLY HATED HAVING HER PUT TO DEATH.
THANK YOU, QUEEN MAUD--

HEY--
BEGGING YOUR PARDON, O BEAUTIFUL QUEEN!
WE CAME AS QUICKLY AS WE COULD, YOUR MAJESTY. AT LEAST I DID, HE SAID HE WAS TIRED. TIRED, I SAID? HOW CAN YOU BE SO TIRED --

SILENCE! WHY AREN'T YOU OUT EXPANDING OUR TERRITORY? -- AND LOOK AT HOW FILTHY YOUR TAILS ARE!

WE'VE BEEN SO BUSY ... IT SLIPPED OUR MINDS ... BUT NOW THAT YOU MENTION IT ...
WE'VE BEEN VERY BUSY EXPANDING OUR TERRITORY AS YOU COMMANDED, BUT WE HAVE COME TO REPORT AN ODD PHENOMENON -- MAMMALS FALLING FROM THE SKY!

MAMMALS FROM THE SKY? THAT'S CERTAINLY DIFFERENT! WHERE ARE THEY?
ESCAPED, MY QUEEN!
I STILL HAVE A STITCH IN MY SIDE FROM CHASING THEM.

SOMETHING DOESN'T SEEM RIGHT HERE.
SEND OUT A HUNTING PARTY AND BRING THESE CREATURES TO ME ...

...WHO KNOWS WHAT KIND OF TROUBLE MAMMALS THAT FALL FROM THE SKY COULD CAUSE.

AND THAT'S HOW I MANAGED TO CATCH FIVE HUNDRED MUSKRATS WITH ONLY A SINGLE RAISIN!

YOU GOTTA BE THE BEST TRAPPER EVER - - WHAT'S A TRAPPER?
GOOD QUESTION.

A TRAPPER IS A UNIQUE INDIVIDUAL THAT CAPTURES WILD CRITTERS FOR A VARIETY OF REASONS. SOMETIMES FOR FOOD, SOMETIMES TO MAKE CLOTHIN'...

SOMETIMES IT'S JUST TO LET THE VARMINTS KNOW WHO'S TH' SMARTEST SON-OF-A-SHE-WOLF WHO EVER WALKED ON TWO LEGS!
THAT'S ME. IN CASE YOU HAVEN'T GUESSED.
GAK! ACK!

THAT'S WHY I DO IT, YEP! I LIKE TO SHOW 'EM WHO'S BOSS!
THAT'S JUST LOVELY. SO TELL ME, WHAT MAKES YOU ANY DIFFERENT FROM THE RAT CREATURES WHO ARE ATTACKING US?!
WELL, FOR ONE THING, I'M ON YOUR SIDE!

WHAT ABOUT THE RAT CREATURES? ARE YOU GONNA SHOW THEM WHO'S BOSS AND GET OUR MOMMAS AND POPPAS BACK - - ARE YOU?
I DON'T BELIEVE I'VE EVER TRAPPED A RAT CREATURE BEFORE . . .

WAIT! I DON'T KNOW IF IT'S SUCH A GOOD IDEA TO HAVE BIG JOHNSON BONE STIRRING UP TROUBLE!
I THINK WE SHOULD WAIT FOR THE DRAGON FROM THE HIGH COUNCIL TO GET HERE!

WELL, I DON'T HONESTLY KNOW IF THERE'S MUCH WE CAN DO ABOUT YOUR MOMMAS AN' POPPAS . . .
BUT WAITIN' AROUND SURE AIN'T GOIN' TO TEACH THEM MONSTERS WHO'S BOSS!
TAP! TAP!

I REALLY MUST PROTEST, MR. BONE- -
WAITIN' AROUND JES' MAKE YOU EASIER TO CATCH, STILLMAN. WHAT WE GOTTA DO IS TAKE THE FIGHT TO THE RAT CREATURES - -
- - AND KICK SOME SERIOUS TAIL!
THAT'S A TERRIBLE IDEA!

. . . WE AGREE, LITTLE MAMMAL . . .
. . . . A TERRIBLE IDEA, INDEED . . . .
LITTLE MAMMAL? WHO SAID THAT? THE NAME'S BIG JOHNSON BONE! WHAT, YOU COME IN LATE OR SOMETHIN'? STEP OUT INTA TH' LIGHT SO'S I CAN SEE YA!

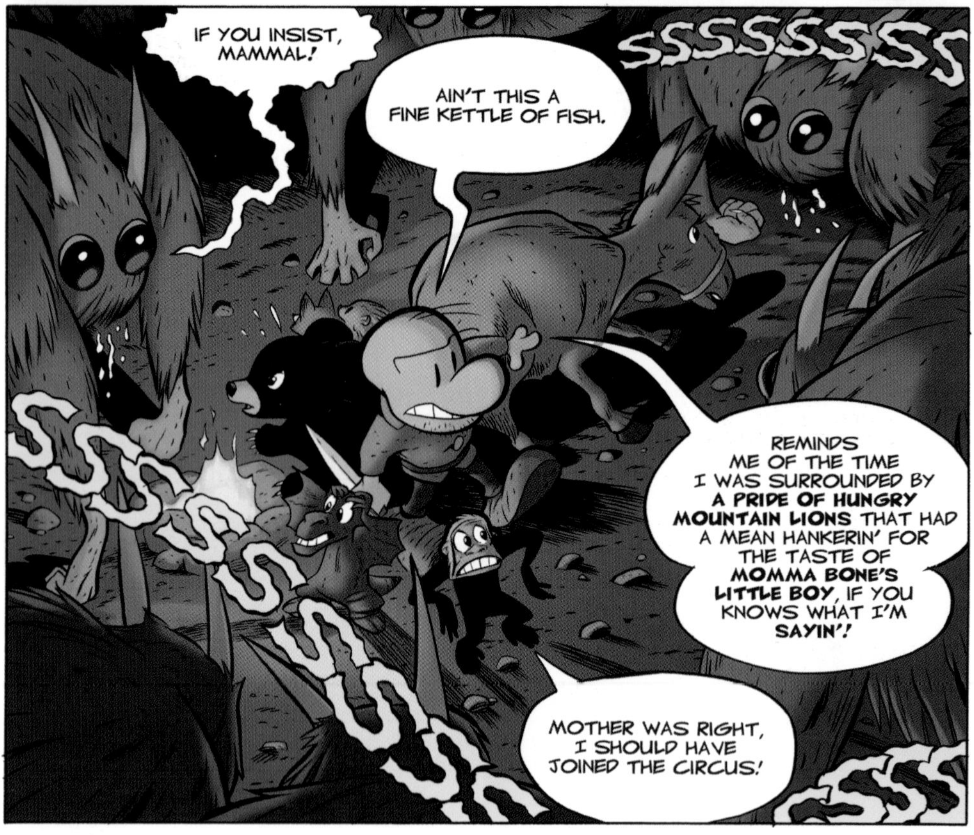
IF YOU INSIST, MAMMAL!
SSSSSSSSS
AIN'T THIS A FINE KETTLE OF FISH.
REMINDS ME OF THE TIME I WAS SURROUNDED BY A PRIDE OF HUNGRY MOUNTAIN LIONS THAT HAD A MEAN HANKERIN' FOR THE TASTE OF MOMMA BONE'S LITTLE BOY, IF YOU KNOWS WHAT I'M SAYIN'!
MOTHER WAS RIGHT, I SHOULD HAVE JOINED THE CIRCUS!

The Lost Tale of BIG JOHNSON BONE
WE'RE SURROUNDED BY RAT CREATURES!
NOBODY PANIC!
WHERE WAS I? OH, YEAH, SO THERE I WAS, MY BACK PRESSED AGAINST A COLD CAVE WALL AND FOUR OF THE HUNGRIEST-LOOKIN' MOUNTAIN LIONS I EVER SEEN COMIN' RIGHT AT ME! YOU LISTENIN', MR. POOT?
FOR THE HUNDRETH TIME TODAY, IT'S PIP! MR. PIP! NOW SAVE ME!!
RIGHT! WELL, I KNEW THEM CATS WOULD BE ON ME LIKE SLIPPERY ON BUTTER - -
EEK!
RUN! IT'S OUR ONLY CHANCE!
- - USIN' SKILLS TAUGHT TO ME BY THE ANCIENT AND MYSTERIOUS HOWTHEHECKAREYA TRIBE - -
I MADE MY MOVE!
HISSSS!

HISSS!
I'M NOT SURE IF YOU'RE AWARE OF THIS, BUT THE TAIL WAS ADDED TO THE CREATURES OF THE WILD DURIN' CREATION SO'S I'D HAVE SOMETHIN' TO GRAB ON TO!

THAT'S A FACT! THE POWERS THAT BE THEMSELVES FILLED ME IN ON THAT ONE!
AAAIIIEEEE!
NOT SO ROUGH!
GO! GO!

BAM!
WAAGH!
oooh!
YOU DO REALIZE THAT HE'S CERTIFIABLY INSANE.

MY, AREN'T YOU THE TASTIEST LITTLE MAMMALS I EVER DID SEE?
ONE STEP CLOSER, AND I'LL BASH YOUR HEAD IN!
START BASHIN'! START BASHIN'!
WHO'S BASHIN'?

HELP MEEE!
DO YOU HEAR THAT? SOUNDS PAINFUL --
AND COMING THIS WAY!

AAAAH!
I'M SO EMBARRASSED!

WHAM CRUNCH!
OUCH! BET THAT'LL SCAR.
SO WHAT SHOULD WE DO?
WOULD YOU LOOK AT THOSE POOR SLOBS?

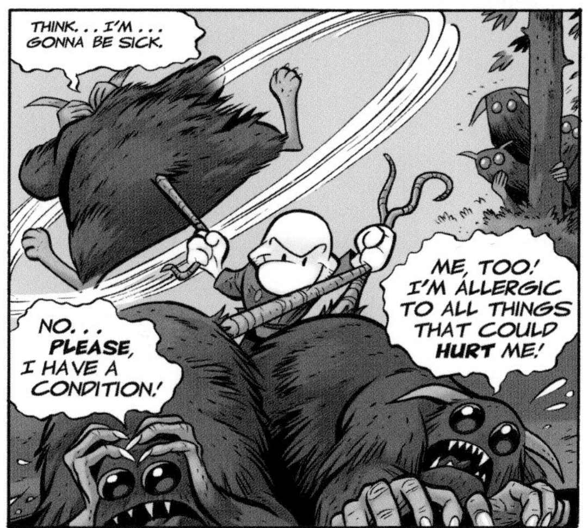
THINK. . . I'M . . . GONNA BE SICK.
NO. . . PLEASE, I HAVE A CONDITION!
ME, TOO! I'M ALLERGIC TO ALL THINGS THAT COULD HURT ME!

OH, DEAR, GET A HOLD OF YOURSELF, STILLMAN -- YOU'RE A PROTECTOR DRAGON FOR PETE'S SAKE. NO WONDER THE HIGH COUNCIL OF DRAGONS WANTS TO REPLACE YOU!

FASTER, BIG JOHNSON! SWING 'EM FASTER!
THAT OUGHTA TEACH 'EM NOT TO PICK ON US!
IF IT WASN'T FOR THE PUKING, I'D SAY THAT LOOKS LIKE FUN!

WAUGH!
GLOOOB
YIIII!
YEP, I JUST GRABBED 'EM BY THE TAILS AND STARTED SPINNIN'!
NOT ONLY DID I SWING FORTY LIONS OVER MY HEAD, BUT I FINISHED UP A NICE LEATHER BELT I'D BEEN WORKIN' ON.

I CAN'T STAND THE SCREAMING ANYMORE, WE HAVE TO DO SOMETHING!
I THOUGHT IT WAS ONLY FOUR MOUNTAIN LIONS.
AND WHERE DID THE BELT COME FROM, HE NEVER MENTIONED A BELT.

EAT ROCK, RATS!

...THE VERY SAME BELT I USED TO TIE OFF MY BLEEDIN' STUMP WHEN MY ARM GOT TORN OFF --

WHOOPS!
KRAK!

I'M FREE! I'M FLYING!!
OH, LOOK, THE GROUND IS COMING UP TO MEET ME.

QUICKLY! LET US GET TO OUR FEET, COMRADE.
THANK YOU, THANK YOU SO MUCH. HAVE I EVER TOLD YOU HOW SPECIAL YOU ARE TO ME?
I HAVE SEEN THE FACE OF TERROR AND IT IS THE BIG JOHNSON BONE.

BIG JOHNSON! ARE YOU ALL RIGHT?
NEVER BETTER, MY DEAR, AND MIGHT I ADD THAT IS QUITE THE STUNNING FROCK YOU'RE WEARING THIS EVENING!
UH, OH.
WHAT HAVE I DONE?

INTO THE WOODS BEFORE THE BIG JOHNSON BONE REGAINS HIS SENSES!
WE CANNOT RETURN TO OUR QUEEN EMPTY-HANDED!
HELP!
I DON'T WANT TO GO IN THE SACK!

THEY'RE TAKING LILY AND PETE - - THIS IS AWFUL!
AH, SWEET GWENDOLYN! WHEN I'M WITH YOU ALL'S RIGHT WITH THE WORLD. ONE, TWO-THREE, ONE, TWO-THREE . . .
WHAT'S WRONG WITH HIM?
HAS HE BEEN DRINKING?
THEY'RE GETTING AWAY!

HACK!
COUGH! COUGH!

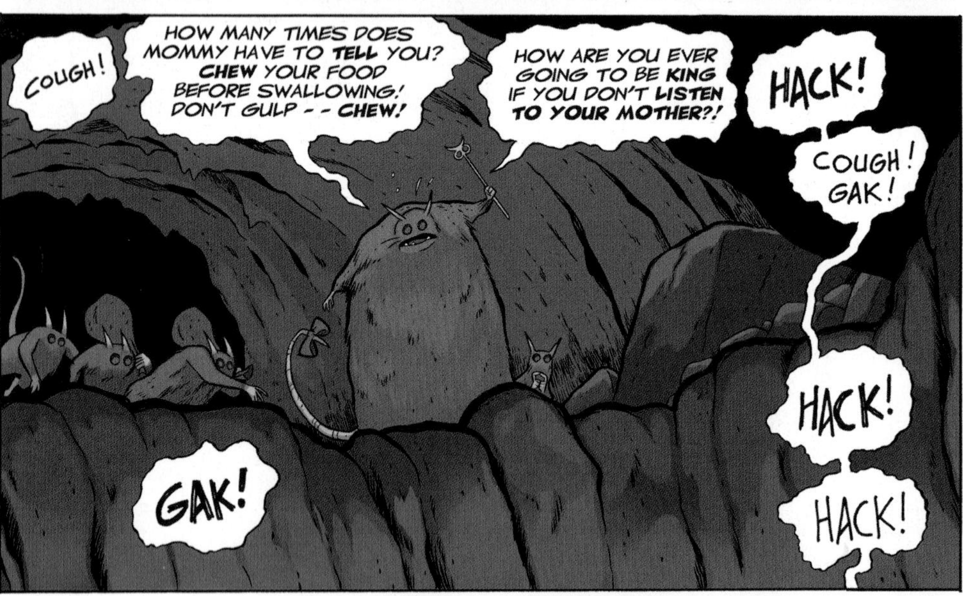
COUGH!
HOW MANY TIMES DOES MOMMY HAVE TO TELL YOU? CHEW YOUR FOOD BEFORE SWALLOWING! DON'T GULP - - CHEW!
HOW ARE YOU EVER GOING TO BE KING IF YOU DON'T LISTEN TO YOUR MOTHER?!
HACK!
COUGH! GAK!
HACK!
GAK!
HACK!

KIDS . . . WHAT'RE YA GONNA DO? SO, WHAT HAVE YOU BROUGHT ME? IT BETTER BE THOSE ANIMALS THAT FELL FROM THE SKY.
SORT OF, O BEAUTEOUS QUEEN - -

. . .THEIR LEADER MANAGED TO ESCAPE. . .
HIS NAME IS BIG JOHNSON BONE, AN' HE KICKED YOUR TAILS BUT GOOD!
YOU TELL 'EM, LILY!

THERE'S NOTHING SPECIAL ABOUT THESE LITTLE ANIMALS! WHO'S THIS BIG JOHNSON BONE?
LET ME EXPLAIN, MY MERCIFUL QUEEN . . .
NOTHING SPECIAL? I CAN BURP THE ALPHABET!

THE BIG JOHNSON BONE FIGHTS LIKE TEN DRAGONS! HE SWUNG US BY OUR TAILS!
BY YOUR TAILS?! WHAT KIND OF A MONSTER IS THIS?
THAT IS SO COOL.
A-B-

HE THOUGHT OUR TAILS WERE HANDLES PUT THERE FOR HIS OWN USE!
AAH! HORRORS!! THIS BEAST MUST BE FOUND AT ALL COSTS BEFORE HE RUINS MY PLANS TO OVERRUN THE VALLEY!

WE ONLY WANT CREATURES WHO HAVE THE PROPER RESPECT FOR OUR TAILS TO BE OUR SLAVES!
THIS CALLS FOR STRONGER MEASURES!

OH, TYSON, DEAR, HOW WOULD MOTHER'S LITTLE PRINCE LIKE TO GO CRUSH SOME NASTY LITTLE MAMMALS THAT ARE GIVING MOMMY A MIGRAINE?
MAMMALS GIVE MOMMY MIGRAINES?! GAH! TYSON PUNISH BAD MAMMALS! BAD, BAD BAD MAMMALS!
WHOA! WOULD YA LOOK AT THE SIZE OF HIM?
!
HACK!
COFF!

YOU SURE IT WASN'T A PIECE OF THE MOON?
I'M SURE. WHO'S GWENDOLYN?
THIS IS TERRIBLE! TERRIBLE!

I'LL SAY IT'S TERRIBLE. THE RATS TOOK THE TWO BEST FRIENDS WE EVER HAD!
PETE AND LILY-- I MISS 'EM ALREADY.
DID YOU SEE THE SIZE OF TH' PELTS ON THEM BEASTIES?
HOO-DAWGIES!

THAT'S THE KIND OF THING THAT SETS A TRAPPER'S BLOOD AFIRE!
WHAT ARE YOU TALKING ABOUT?

PICTURE IT, MR. POOP: A FANCY LADY BONE WEARING A RAT CREATURE FUR COAT - - OR A SMILING GENTLE-BONE WEARING A LARGE FUR HAT WITH A LONG RAT CREATURE TAIL DRAGGING ON THE GROUND BEHIND HIM!
SICK!
OH, MY.

- - OR BETTER YET - - A BIG, FAT BONE BITING INTO A RAT CREATURE SANDWICH! THEM THERE SMELLY VARMINTS COULD BE THE NEXT BEST THING TO STRIKING GOLD!

BUT, MR. BONE, WHAT ABOUT LILY AND PETE? YOU'RE GOING TO SAVE THEM, AREN'T YOU?
OF COURSE I'M GONNA SAVE 'EM, RAMONA! I'M BIG JOHNSON BONE FOR CRYIN' OUT LOUD!
Hmf!

AND HOW DO WE RESCUE TWO KIDS FROM THE CLUTCHES OF MULTIPLE FLESH-EATING MONSTERS?
QUITE SIMPLE, MR. PLOP! TH' SAME WAY I DID WHEN I RESCUED THE BEAUTIFUL QUEEN HOO-HAA FROM THE CLUTCHES OF FLESH-EATING OGRES!
HE'S INSANE! AND IT'S ALL MY FAULT FOR THROWING THAT ROCK!

QUIT BEATIN' YERSELF UP, STILLMAN. WHY DON'T YOU USE THAT ENERGY TO HELP ME GET THOSE KIDS BACK?
ME?
HELP YOU? HOW? I CAN'T BREATHE FIRE WITHOUT THROWING UP.

DON'T FRET NOW, EACH AN' EVERY ONE OF YOU WILL PLAY AN IMPORTANT PART IN MY INGENIOUS PLAN FOR THE LIBERATION OF PETE AND LILY!
OH, NOW THAT'S ENOUGH! THEY'RE JUST CHILDREN! WHAT KIND OF HELP COULD THEY BE?
I'M VERY SMALL.

I'D SAY YOU LOST YOUR MIND A LONG TIME AGO, BUT YOU'D PROBABLY HAVE SOME RIDICULOUS STORY ABOUT HOW YOU LOST YOUR SANITY AND FOUND IT AGAIN ON ONE OF THE TALLEST MOUNTAIN PEAKS IN THE WORLD- -

IN ACTUALITY, I LOST IT PROSPECTIN' FOR GOLD IN THE FROZEN NORTH, BUT FOUND IT WITH THE HELP OF A KINDLY SHERPA NAMED BENNY- -
- - BUT THAT'S A STORY FOR ANOTHER TIME! WE GOT US SOME KIDS TO RESCUE.
BINK!

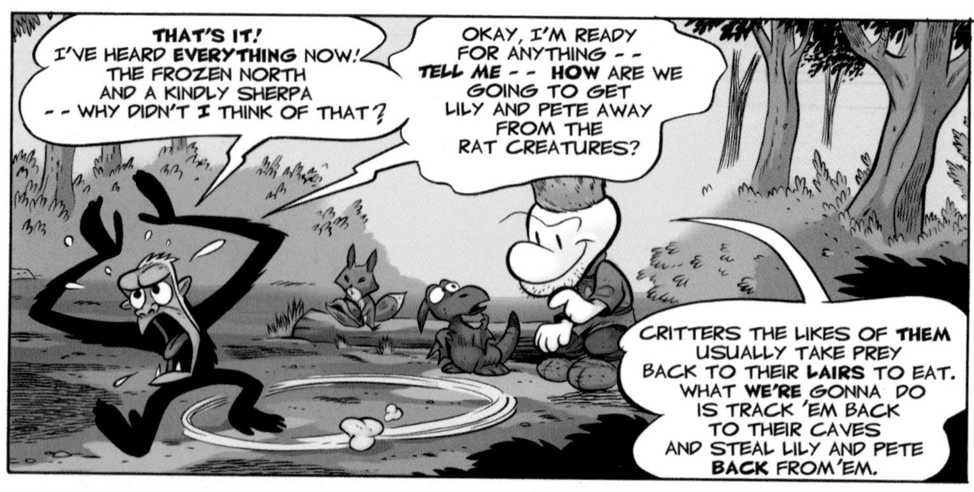
THAT'S IT! I'VE HEARD EVERYTHING NOW! THE FROZEN NORTH AND A KINDLY SHERPA - - WHY DIDN'T I THINK OF THAT?
OKAY, I'M READY FOR ANYTHING - - TELL ME - - HOW ARE WE GOING TO GET LILY AND PETE AWAY FROM THE RAT CREATURES?
CRITTERS THE LIKES OF THEM USUALLY TAKE PREY BACK TO THEIR LAIRS TO EAT. WHAT WE'RE GONNA DO IS TRACK 'EM BACK TO THEIR CAVES AND STEAL LILY AND PETE BACK FROM 'EM.

BUT- - WE GOTTA BE EXTRA QUIET ON ACCOUNT OF VARMINTS CAN BE EXTREMELY DANGEROUS IF INTERRUPTED WHILE THEY'S ALREADY EATIN'!
OKAY, NOW WHO WANTS TO GO WITH ME?

WHAT? SOMEBODY GOT A BETTER PLAN? LET'S HEAR IT, THEN - - AND IF IT INVOLVES TWENTY POUNDS OF BACON FAT AND A HOT-AIR BALLOON, I CAN TELL YA RIGHT NOW, IT AIN'T GONNA WORK.

WE'RE AFRAID, BIG JOHNSON. THE RAT CREATURES HAVE BEEN THE TERRORS OF THIS VALLEY SINCE BEFORE WE WERE BORN. SERIOUSLY, WHAT KIND OF A CHANCE WOULD WE HAVE?

WELL, NOW... THEM STUPID RAT-TAILS AIN'T NOTHIN' TO BE AFRAID OF... BUT I UNDERSTAND.
YOU MAY FIND THIS HARD TO SWALLA, BUT EVEN BIG JOHNSON BONE WAS AFRAID ONCE. IT'S TRUE.

IT HAPPENED WHEN I WAS A YOUNG EXPLORER-- NO, WAIT... I'D JUST TURNED THE AGE OF- - NO, NO - -UH... WELL, I CAN'T RIGHTLY RECALL THE INCIDENT, BUT I'M SURE I WAS A-SCARED ONCET!
hMM.

Y'SEE, FEAR IS LIKE A BIG OL' ANIMAL - - I SEEN IT BLEND WITH THE SCENERY AND POUNCE ON YA BEFORE YOU KNOWS IT WAS EVEN THERE!
FEAR CAN MAKE IT SO'S YOU DON'T EVEN WANT TO KNOW WHAT LIES OVER THAT NEXT BIG HILL ON ACCOUNT A NOT WANTIN' TO BE A-SCARED AGAIN. AN' THAT'S BAD, IF YOU'RE A EXPLORER LIKE ME.

SO YOU GOTTA DECIDE! ARE YOU GONNA LET BEING AFRAID KEEP YOU FROM EXPLORING? OR YOU GONNA SLAP A MUZZLE ON IT AN' GO?

'COURSE, MAYBE YOU ALL ALREADY MADE YOUR DECISIONS...
RIGHT! YOU STAY HERE, AND I'LL SEE ABOUT GETTIN' THEM YOUNGINS BACK.
MR. BONE?

I'M TIRED OF BEING SCARED. I WANT TO PUT A MUZZLE ON IT AND GO WITH YOU. I WANT MY FRIENDS BACK!
BUT, PORTER, THE RAT CREATURES, YOU CAN'T...

I CAN!! SOMEBODY GO AND GET ME A STICK!

WHY DO I GET THE FEELING THIS IS WHERE ALL RATIONAL THOUGHT GOES OUT THE WINDOW?

HURRY, GIRLS . . .
MAY I SAY YOU LOOK **LOVELY** FOR YOUR SPEECH TODAY, QUEEN MAUD! YOUR PEOPLE AWAIT YOU . . .
YES, QUEEN MAUD.
IT'S A SIN REALLY, ALL THIS BEAUTY GOING TO WASTE ON MATTERS OF STATE. . . BUT THEN I'D HAVE TO FIND SOMEBODY WHO COULD LIVE UP TO THE STANDARDS OF MY DEARLY DEPARTED HUSBAND. . .

HE WAS A **BEAUT**, THAT ONE WAS. SOME DAYS I REALLY DO MISS HIM . . .
BUT THEN THERE ARE DAYS LIKE **THIS** WHEN I GET TO DO THE **QUEEN** THING - -
RAH!
- - AND I WISH HE'D EATEN THAT BAD PORK SOONER!
RAH! RAH!

MY SUBJECTS! YOUR QUEEN HAS **NEED** OF YOU!
YAAY!
HUZZAH!

STRANGE CREATURES HAVE INVADED THE VALLEY - -
CREATURES WHO DO NOT RESPECT THE BEAUTY OF OUR **TAILS!!**
GASP!

WITH THE HELP OF MY BELOVED SON - -
YOU WILL **DESTROY** THESE INVADERS SO THAT **WE MAY INVADE!**
ME AM GONNA PUNISH BAD MAMMALS...
COUGH.

WHY SHOULD **WE** HIDE IN DANK, DARK CAVES WHILE **THEY** THRIVE IN THE BOUNTIFUL, SUN-WARMED FORESTS?

OUR TIME HAS COME, SO MAKE ME **PROUD!**
NOW, GO! DESTROY THE BIG JOHNSON BONE!!
HOORAH!

HEY!
UNNGH!
WAIT FOR ME! ME AM THE QUEEN'S SON, Y'KNOW!
COFF!
WAIT! ME STUCK!
HACK. COUGH
HEY!

DON'T FORGET ME!
I DON'T WANT TO BE AFRAID ANYMORE EITHER! I WANT TO GO WITH YOU!
I CAN'T BELIEVE THIS IS HAPPENING!

I HOPE YOU'RE HAPPY, JOHNSON! NOW ALL THESE POOR BABY ANIMALS WILL GO TO THEIR DEATHS WITH YOU!
NOBODY'S GONNA DIE. I'LL SEE TO THAT!
LET ME AT 'EM!

I'VE COMPLETELY LOST CONTROL HERE! NO WONDER THE HIGH COUNCIL OF DRAGONS PUT ME ON PROBATION!
RAMONA! HE'S TAKING YOU TO THE RAT CREATURES! HELLO?! REMEMBER? LARGE TEETH AND CLAWS?
I THINK I NEED A STICK, TOO - - A BIG ONE!

C'MON NOW, GANG. WE'RE WASTIN' TIME HERE. LET'S GET A MOVE ON.
ARE YOU SURE THIS IS THE BEST PLAN YOU CAN COME UP WITH? I'D FEEL ONLY A TAD WORSE IF YOU SUGGESTED WE ALL MARCH OFF A CLIFF.

I NEED YOU AN' BLOSSOM TO STAY HERE WITH THE MICE AN' THE DRAGON, MR. POP.
IF SOMETHIN' DOES HAPPEN TO US, I WANT SOMEBODY AROUND THAT COULD TELL THE TALE OF WHAT HAPPENED TO BIG JOHNSON BONE WHEN HE WENT UP AGAINST THE FEARSOME RAT CREATURES.
I CAN HANDLE THAT.

THIS IS MADNESS! MADNESS, I TELL YOU!
I'M STILL THE GUARDIAN OF THIS PART OF THE FOREST! I FORBID YOU TO GO!
PLEASE DON'T GO!
GET A HOLD OF YERSELF, STILLMAN.

YOU GOT NOTHIN' TO WORRY ABOUT. WE'LL BE BACK BEFORE YOU EVEN START MISSIN' US.
I JUST DON'T WANT YOU TO BE KILLED.

NOW DON'T YOU WORRY ABOUT US. BESIDES -- I ALREADY BEEN DEAD ONCET -- DIDN'T CARE FOR IT A BIT. ADIOS!
ADIOS!

THEY'RE REALLY GOING!
MAYBE THEY'LL BE ALL RIGHT... MAYBE THEY'LL MARCH RIGHT INTO THOSE CAVES AND SAVE THOSE KIDS AND... AND.....

...AND IT SOUNDS SO MUCH MORE CREDIBLE WHEN BIG JOHNSON SAYS IT. I ALMOST BELIEVE IT COULD HAPPEN.
ALMOST.

BUT, BIG JOHNSON, HOW DID YOU GET OUT FROM UNDER ALL THAT SNOW FROM THE AVALANCHE?
WELL, RAMONA, I REALLY GOT A THING FOR **SOUP** - -

LIKING **SOUP** GOT YOU OUTTA A AVALANCHE? HOW?

USE YER COCONUT, SON. IF A MAN LIKES HIS SOUP THEN HE **GOTTA** HAVE HIS SOUP-EATIN' **ACCOUTREMENTS** WITH HIM AT ALL TIMES!
YOU USED A **SPOON** TO TUNNEL YOUR WAY OUT OF THE SNOW?

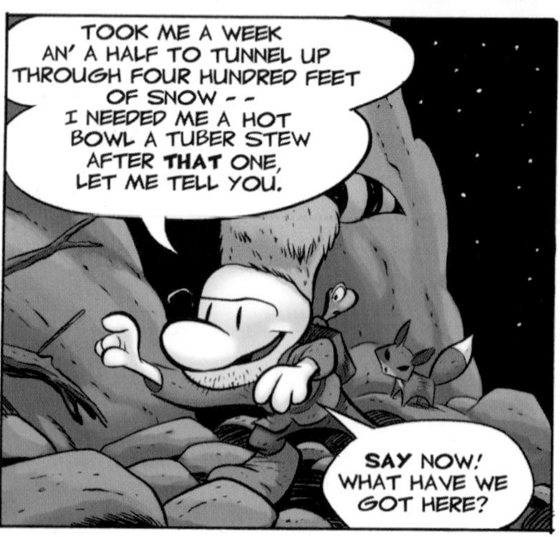
TOOK ME A WEEK AN' A HALF TO TUNNEL UP THROUGH FOUR HUNDRED FEET OF SNOW - - I NEEDED ME A HOT BOWL A TUBER STEW AFTER **THAT** ONE, LET ME TELL YOU.
SAY NOW! WHAT HAVE WE GOT HERE?

IT'S A **PORCUPINE QUILL!** WE'RE ON THE RIGHT TRAIL!
OL' PETE!
HANG ON, PETE AN' LILY! **WE'RE COMING!**

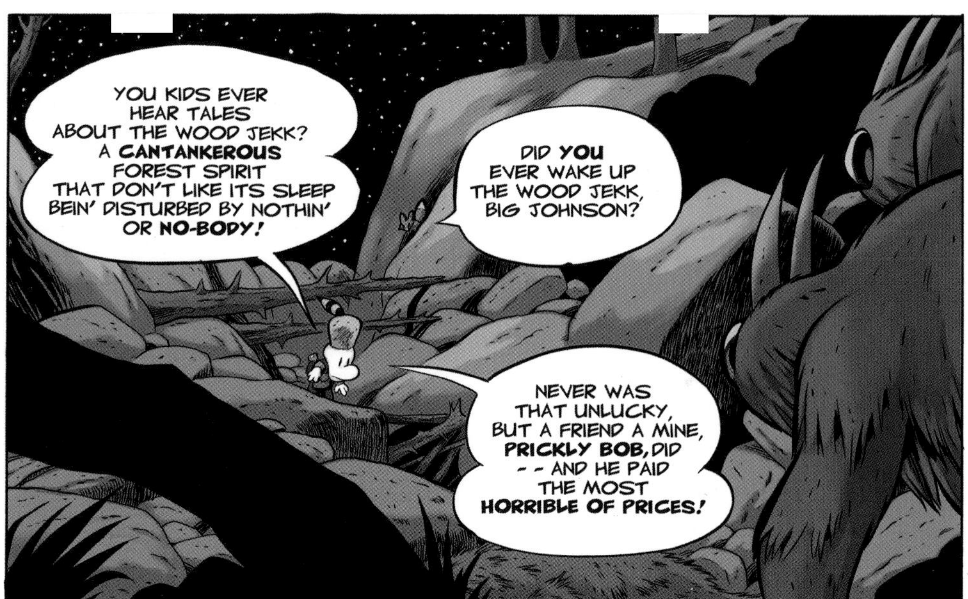
YOU KIDS EVER HEAR TALES ABOUT THE WOOD JEKK? A CANTANKEROUS FOREST SPIRIT THAT DON'T LIKE ITS SLEEP BEIN' DISTURBED BY NOTHIN' OR NO-BODY!
DID YOU EVER WAKE UP THE WOOD JEKK, BIG JOHNSON?
NEVER WAS THAT UNLUCKY, BUT A FRIEND A MINE, PRICKLY BOB, DID -- AND HE PAID THE MOST HORRIBLE OF PRICES!

THEY SAY PRICKLY BOB WENT OFF INTA THE WOODS AN' STUMBLED OVER THE WOOD JEKK -- -- AND HE NEVER CAME BACK!

DID... DID THEY... DID THEY EVER FIND HIM?
YEAH, DID PRICKLY BOB EVER COME BACK?
OH, THEY FOUND HIM ALL RIGHT...

BUT HIS HEAD HAD BEEN REPLACED BY A CANTALOUPE!!

ARRAGH! PRICKLY BOB LOST HIS HEAD!
YAAGGH! WHAT'S A CANTALOUPE?!

RAT CREATURES!
FOLLOW 'EM!
THEY CAN TAKE US TO PETE AND LILY!
AAIEE! IT'S THE WOOD JEKK!
RUN! OR WE'LL END UP LIKE PRICKLY BOB!

BOMP!

WELL, SHAVE MY LEGS AN' CALL ME BETSY - -
HACK!
COUGH.

- - DIDN'T THINK THEY GREW 'EM THAT BIG.
HELLO? ARE YOU THE BAD MAMMALS THAT GIVE MOMMY MIGRAINES?
HACK
COUGH

IT'S A WONDER THE HIGH COUNCIL DIDN'T FIRE ME SOONER! WHAT AM I, A MOUSE NO OFFENSE ? HOW COULD I LET THIS HAPPEN? THOSE ANIMALS WERE MY RESPONSIBILITY.
GIVE IT A REST, STILLMAN. THEY'LL EITHER COME BACK OR THEY WON'T. THERE'S NOTHING YOU CAN DO ABOUT IT.

NO, MR. PIP. THAT'S WHERE YOU'RE WRONG!

IT'S LIKE BIG JOHNSON SAID, YOU HAVE TO DECIDE WHETHER OR NOT BEING AFRAID IS GOING TO RUN YOUR LIFE - -
WELL, I'VE DECIDED!
BEING AFRAID DOESN'T RUN MY LIFE - - IT JUST OFFERS VALUABLE GUIDELINES. MARCHING STRAIGHT INTO THE RAT CREATURES' CAVE IS IDIOTIC!

IDIOTIC OR NOT, IT'S TIME I STARTED ACTING LIKE A GUARDIAN DRAGON! YOU COMING WITH ME OR NOT?

BLOSSOM? WHERE ON EARTH DO YOU THINK YOU'RE GOING?! BIG JOHNSON GAVE US SPECIFIC INSTRUCTIONS TO STAY HERE - -
FINE! BE THAT WAY! BUT I WOULDN'T WANT TO BE YOU WHEN HE FINDS OUT THAT NOBODY KNOWS HOW HE DIED!

MAMMALS THAT CAUSE MIGRAINES? WELL, THAT'S NOT US. WE'RE NOT MAMMALS - - NO SIR! WE'RE . . . UH . . . WE'RE COLD BLOODED. AIN'T THAT RIGHT, KIDS?
YEP, WE'RE AMPHIBIANS THROUGH AN' THROUGH!
HEE HEE HEE

AMPHIBIANS?
UH, OKAY, IF YOU SEE THE BAD MAMMALS, YOU TELL THEM TYSON LOOKIN' FOR THEM.

WILL DO! YOU TAKE CARE, NOW!
WE'LL JUST RUN ALONG AN' FIND A LAKE SO'S WE CAN BREATHE IN IT. LET'S GO, GUYS.

BYE-BYE, LITTLE AMPHIBIANS. HAVE A GOOD SWIM.

GOING SOMEWHERE, SMALL MAMMALS?
SSSSSSS
ANYBODY EVER TOLD YOU GUYS THAT YOU'RE A PAIN IN THE BUTT?

SMALL MAMMALS?
AMPHIBIANS LIED TO TYSON!

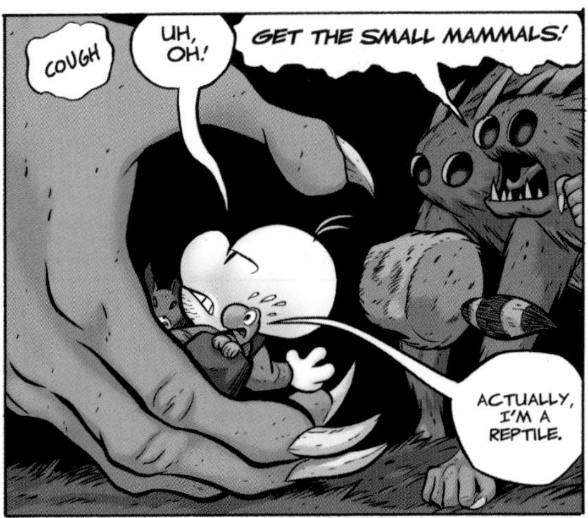
COUGH
UH, OH!
GET THE SMALL MAMMALS!
ACTUALLY, I'M A REPTILE.

TRY TO THINK OF THIS AS AN OPPORTUNITY FOR ADVENTURE, KIDS!
I'D LIKE THE OPPORTUNITY TO STAY ALIVE!

BANZAI!
WHO DARES ATTACK HER MAJESTY'S CRACK TROOPS?!

I DARE!
STILLMAN -- FORMERLY OF THE GUARDIAN DRAGONS! RELEASE OUR FRIENDS IMMEDIATELY!

YOU ARE TOO LATE! LOOK!
I'M A LITTLE TEAPOT... SHORT AND STOUT...

EEK!
DON'T PANIC, RAMONA! YOU MAY FIND THIS HARD TO BELIEVE, BUT I GOT THE SITUATION UNDER CONTROL!

HANG ON, BIG JOHNSON! HANG ON!
I TOLD YOU THIS WOULD END BADLY, DIDN'T I? BUT NO -- NOBODY LISTENS TO THE MONKEY!

THIS REMINDS ME OF THE TIME I WAS ALMOST CONSUMED BY THE VORACIOUS HUNGRISAUR! THERE I WAS, BUCK NAKED AND . . .
YEEEEE!

MM. GOOD!
CLUMP!
HEK COUGH
CAFF!

THEY. . . THEY'RE GONE!
SSSSS
SSSSSSS
CAN I INTEREST ANY OF YOU IN A MONKEY?

The Lost Tale of BIG JOHNSON BONE
oooh
TUMMY...
...TUMMY UPSET!
SQUIRGLE! GURGLE!
JUST LOOK AT YOU! FROM THE LOOKS OF YOUR FLACCID TAIL I WOULD GUESS THAT YOU ATE SOMETHING AND YOU DIDN'T CHEW!
HOW MANY TIMES DOES MOMMY HAVE TO TELL YOU NOT TO GULP YOUR FOOD?!
MOVE! THE QUEEN WANTS A WORD WITH YOU PATHETIC PRISONERS BEFORE YOU MEET YOUR MOST HORRIBLE END!
THIS IS ALL MY FAULT... HOW COULD I LET THE KIDS AND BIG JOHNSON BONE GET EATEN?
YES, QUITE HORRIBLE... I WONDER IF THEY COULD USE A CHEF OF SOME KIND? I MAKE A MEAN STROGANOFF, IF I DO SAY SO MYSELF.
THE PRISONERS, MY QUEEN -- AND NOTICE THAT ONE IS A DRAGON.
AND I, O VISION OF RADIANCE, AM MR. PIP, A LOVESTRUCK SIMIAN WHO WOULD BE HONORED IF HE WERE ALLOWED TO SERVE YOU IN SOME WAY.
DRAGON? MORE LIKE A MOUSE -- NO -- A TEENY, TINY BUG THAT'S SCARED OF DIRT.

I HAVE NO NEED OF MORE SERVANTS, SIMIAN.
NO, NO, I'M LOWER THAN A BUG. WHAT'S LOWER THAN A BUG. . ?
OH, SAY IT ISN'T SO!

IT IS AS I FEARED ON THAT FIRST DAY I HEARD OF YOUR OVERWHELMING BEAUTY - - THAT THERE WOULD BE NO ROOM FOR ME TO WORSHIP AT THE ALTAR OF YOUR LOVELINESS!
YOU HEARD ABOUT MY BEAUTY? I WONDER WHO'S BEEN TALKING?

OF COURSE I DO BELIEVE A GIRL SHOULD ALWAYS TRY TO LOOK HER BEST.
DAMN THESE EYES! IF ONLY THEY HAD NEVER FALLEN UPON YOUR MAGNIFICENCE!
LOWER THAN A BUG, LOWER THAN A BUG...

MY QUEEN, NOT TO INTERRUPT, BUT WHAT IS TO BE DONE WITH THE PRISONERS?
YES, O RAVISHING ONE, WHAT IS TO BECOME OF US? ESPECIALLY ME?

TAKE THEM TO THE PANTRY. WHEN I'M HUNGRY, PREPARE THE MONKEY FIRST. I LIKE HIM.
BUT. . .WAIT! I SAID YOU WERE BEAUTIFUL! YOU THINK THAT WAS EASY?!
A GERM! THAT'S IT! I'M LOWER THAN A GERM!

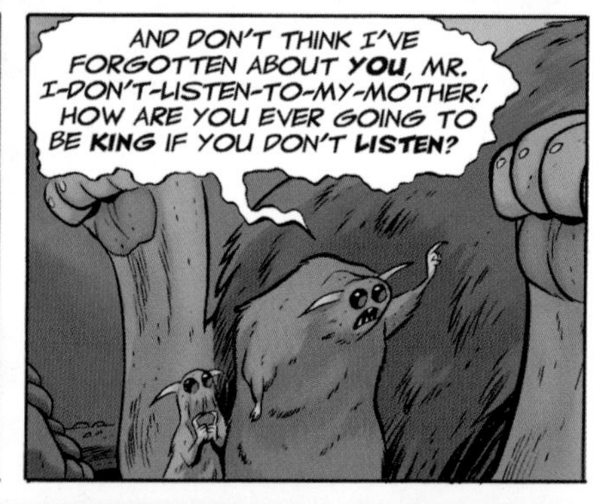
AND DON'T THINK I'VE FORGOTTEN ABOUT YOU, MR. I-DON'T-LISTEN-TO-MY-MOTHER! HOW ARE YOU EVER GOING TO BE KING IF YOU DON'T LISTEN?

CAK! COUGH!
SOMETHING NOT GO DOWN SO GOOD...
BLURRKK!
COUGH! COUGH.
SPLURCHH! RUMBLLE! RUMBLE!

BLURRCH! SQUIRRGLE! BOUMMPH!
BLACKER THAN A CROW'S BACKSIDE IN HERE!
I THINK WE COULD USE SOME ILLUMINATION ON OUR CURRENT PREDICAMENT.
SKRITCH

hmm.

JUST AS I THOUGHT, WE'S INSIDE THE BEASTIE'S FOOD PIPE.
THAT MEANS WE'RE FOOD! I DON'T WANNA BE FOOD!
GET A HOLD OF YOURSELF, RAMONA! BIG JOHNSON WILL THINK OF SOMETHING - - RIGHT, BIG JOHNSON?

RIGHT, PORTER, AN' IF MY RECOLLECTION OF MONSTER ANATOMY DON'T FAIL ME, THE WAY OUTTA HERE IS DOWN!
DOWN?! IF MY RECOLLECTION OF ANATOMY IS RIGHT, DOWN IS EXACTLY WHERE WE DON'T WANT TO GO!

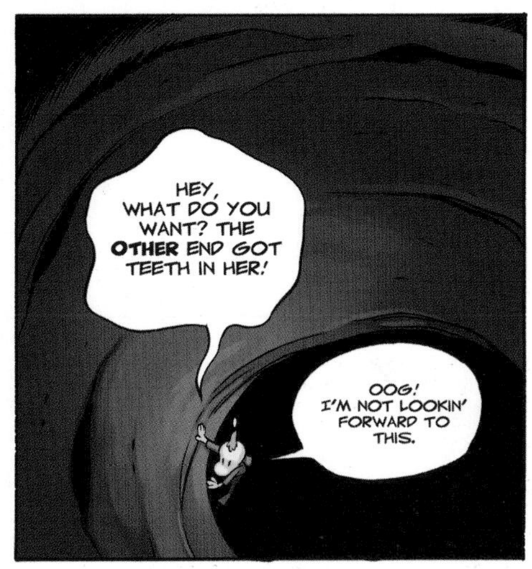
HEY, WHAT DO YOU WANT? THE OTHER END GOT TEETH IN HER!
OOG! I'M NOT LOOKIN' FORWARD TO THIS.

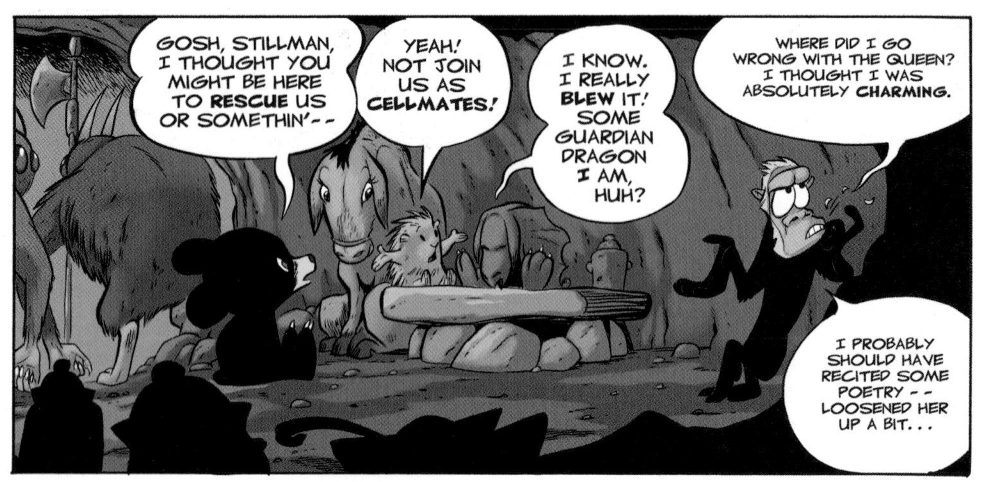
GOSH, STILLMAN, I THOUGHT YOU MIGHT BE HERE TO RESCUE US OR SOMETHIN'--
YEAH! NOT JOIN US AS CELLMATES!
I KNOW. I REALLY BLEW IT! SOME GUARDIAN DRAGON I AM, HUH?
WHERE DID I GO WRONG WITH THE QUEEN? I THOUGHT I WAS ABSOLUTELY CHARMING.
I PROBABLY SHOULD HAVE RECITED SOME POETRY -- LOOSENED HER UP A BIT...

YOUR FATES ARE SEALED, LITTLE ANIMALS -- SO DO NOT WORRY YOURSELVES UNNECESSARILY!
WORRY WILL ONLY TAINT THE TASTE OF YOUR MEAT. SOON, ALL THE ANIMALS IN THE VALLEY WILL BE SWEET MEAT FOR OUR HUNGRY STOMACHS!

WITHOUT A GUARDIAN DRAGON TO PROTECT THEM, ALL THE ANIMALS OF THE VALLEY WILL BE OURS!
I... I THINK I'M GONNA BE... SICK!
ULLURCH!
UH, OH!

FOOMP!!
EXCUSE ME! HOW AM I SUPPOSED TO THINK OF WAYS TO SAVE MY HIDE IF YOU THREE ARE MAKING A RACKET?

WELL, THAT WAS UNEXPECTED.
I THOUGHT HE COULDN'T BREATHE FIRE. I THOUGHT HE JUST THREW STUFF.

CAREFUL!
IT'S AWFUL **SLIPPERY** IN HERE.

BUT NOT AS SLIPPERY AS THE GLACIAL ICE THAT COVERED THE NORTHERN SIDE OF THE ***BIG-BUM-SMACK*** MOUNTAINS!

- -THOSE MOUNTAINS WERE SLIPPERIER THAN **BUTTER THROUGH A GOOSE** - - AND TO MAKE MATTERS **WORSE**, THE ENTIRE MOUNTAIN RANGE WAS PRONE TO - -
LOOK OUT! THE MONSTER IS MOVING!

STOMACH...
...FEEL BAD...
BUURRPPP!

RUMMBLEGRUMBLE!
BLURPP &
BLURRCHHH!
EEK!
EARTH-SHAKES! QUICK! FLAP YOUR ARMS!
WILL THAT HELP?
COULDN'T HURT.

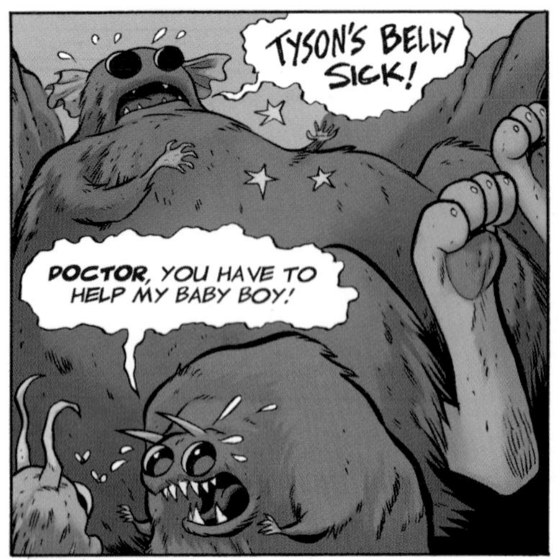
TYSON'S BELLY SICK!
DOCTOR, YOU HAVE TO HELP MY BABY BOY!

WHOA! WOTTA REEK.
NEVER FEAR, MY QUEEN, DOC GUAM IS HERE! I WILL DETERMINE THE CAUSE OF YOUR SON'S DISCOMFORT.
BURRAPP!

YES, YES. GED ON WIT IT!
BAMMPH!

THE PRINCE MAY BE INFECTED WITH ONE OF THE MANY VIRULENT MALADIES THAT INFEST THIS REGION. IT IS GOOD THAT YOU SOUGHT MY EXPERTISE.
PURTTT!

GRRGLLE!
YES, I SEE. THE PRINCE'S AILMENT COULD BE AS SIMPLE AS AN INFLAMED BLUGOSSWICK - - OR AS DEADLY AS A WOOD ELF INFESTATION.
WURRGLLE! BLOOPURCHH!

KNEW A GUY THAT HAD WOOD ELVES - - DIDN'T LAST A MONTH.
PLEASE, DOCTOR, MAKE MY BOY WELL AGAIN!

LET'S HOPE THE BIG FELLA ATE SOMETHING NICE AND SOFT RIGHT BEFORE HE ATE US!
THINK SOFT THOUGHTS, THINK SOFT THOUGHTS...
SPONGE CAKE, SPONGE CAKE, SPONGE CAKE...

DO YOU HEAR SOMETHING? IT ALMOST SOUNDS LIKE RAMONA!
IT'S JUST YOUR EARS PLAYING TRICKS AGAIN, DEAR.
ANYTHING BITING?
NOPE.
SIGH.

LIGHT AS A FEATHER... LIGHT AS A FEATHER...
MARSHMALLOW! MARSHMALLOW! MARSHMALLOW!
SHPLOOP! SPLOP! SPLASH!

WHAT WAS IT? WHAT DID THE MONSTER EAT NOW?
A MONSTER THIS BIG CAN EAT ANYTHING- - SO EVERYBODY STAY BACK UNTIL WE KNOW IT'S FRIENDLY!
SPLASH

MOMMA! POPPA! I KNEW YOU WERE ALIVE!
RAMONA!
BABY!
MA!
SON!

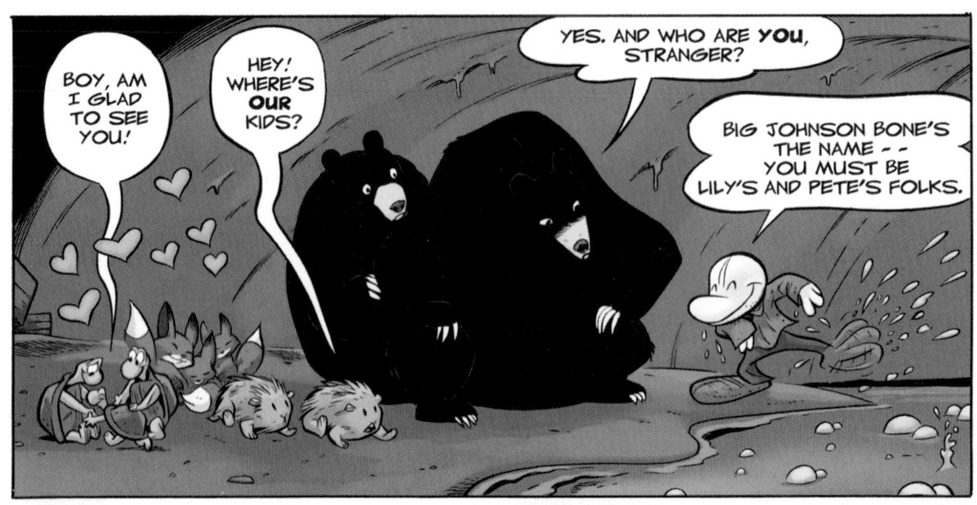
BOY, AM I GLAD TO SEE YOU!
HEY! WHERE'S OUR KIDS?
YES. AND WHO ARE YOU, STRANGER?
BIG JOHNSON BONE'S THE NAME - - YOU MUST BE LILY'S AND PETE'S FOLKS.

THAT'S US! ARE PETE AND LILY ALL RIGHT, MR. BONE?
WELL, IF YOU AIN'T SEEN 'EM, I'D SAY THAT'S A PRETTY GOOD SIGN.

I PLAN ON RESCUIN' THEM NEXT- - JUST AS SOON AS I GET US OUTTA HERE.
?
?
?

YOU DID IT, STILLMAN! I NEVER DOUBTED YOU FOR A MOMENT! WE'RE FREE! NOW LET'S HOT-TAIL IT OUT OF HERE BEFORE SOMEBODY FINDS OUT WE ESCAPED!
WE CAN'T JUST LEAVE, MR. PIP! THE RATS ARE PLANNING TO ATTACK THE VALLEY!

YOU CAN LEAVE IF YOU WANT, BUT I'VE GOT RESPONSIBILITIES. I'M GOING BACK TO DEAL WITH THE QUEEN!
WAIT! I'VE GOT A BETTER IDEA! WE COULD RUN AND HIDE IN THE WOODS! WOULDN'T THAT MAKE THE QUEEN ANGRY-- HIDING AND ALL? ARE YOU LISTENING TO ME!?

SHOULDN'T WE GO AFTER THEM?
I'M AFRAID IF I MOVE-- I'LL CRUMBLE TO DUST.
I DIDN'T EVEN THINK OF THAT.

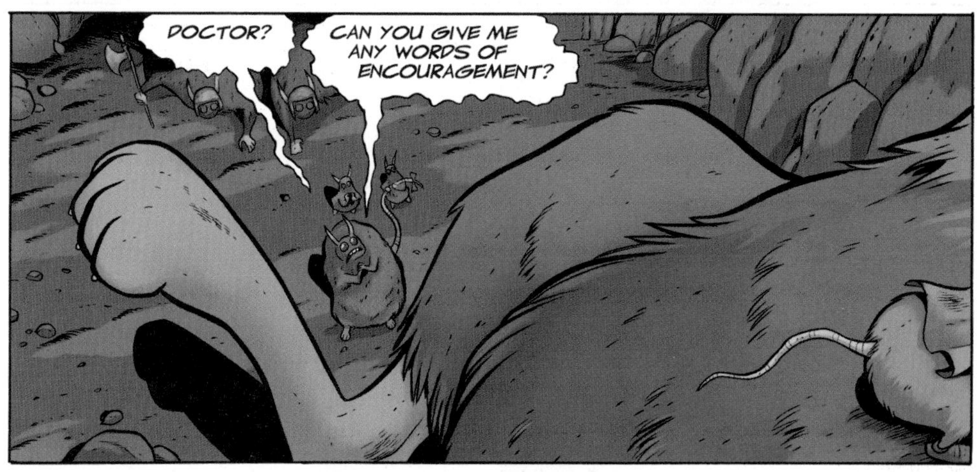
DOCTOR?
CAN YOU GIVE ME ANY WORDS OF ENCOURAGEMENT?

I'VE YET TO COMPLETE THE PHYSICAL EXAMINATION -- BUT I'M LEANING TOWARD THE WOOD ELVES DIAGNOSIS.
BRAAPP!
oohhhhhhhhh!!

YEEEEEE
BEGGING THE QUEEN'S PARDON!
OW! OW! OOTCH! OW!!

GUARD, WHAT IS THE MEANING OF THIS?!
THE DRAGON HAS ESCAPED!
OH, FOR . . . IT'S GOING TO BE ONE OF THOSE DAYS, IS IT?

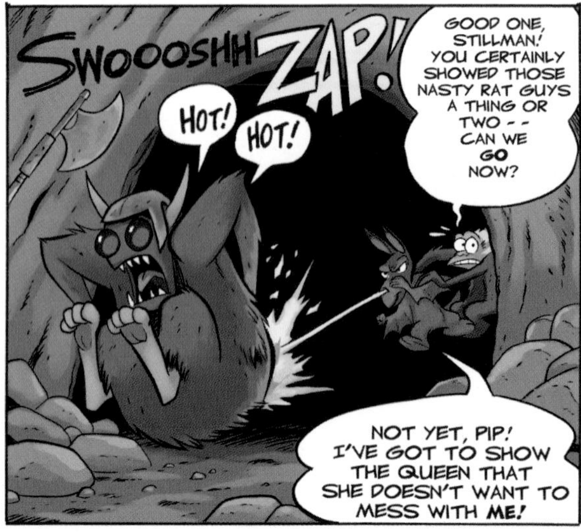
SWOOOSHH
ZAP!
HOT!
HOT!
GOOD ONE, STILLMAN! YOU CERTAINLY SHOWED THOSE NASTY RAT GUYS A THING OR TWO - - CAN WE GO NOW?
NOT YET, PIP! I'VE GOT TO SHOW THE QUEEN THAT SHE DOESN'T WANT TO MESS WITH ME!

I'M NOT LIKING THIS!
YOU WERE CAPTURED ONCE - - WHY DON'T YOU STAY CAPTURED?!

OH, BOY, THAT'S A WHOLE LOTTA RATS.
SILLY ME. I ALMOST BELIEVED THAT I'D LIVE TO SEE ANOTHER DAY.

HELLO?! ANY WOOD ELVES IN THERE?!
HELLO?
COME OUT! COME OUT!

I'VE GOT A LOVELY TREAT FOR ANY WOOD ELVES THAT COME OUT OF THERE RIGHT NOW!
BLURRGLE!
GRUMBLE!
BLURP!
BURROWL!

GRUMBLE! BLURP!
WELL, HOW ABOUT IT, BIG JOHNSON, - - HOW ARE YOU GONNA GET US OUT OF HERE?
I'M WORKIN' ON IT, PORTER, BUT IT'S A BIT CHILLY IN THE BELLY OF THE BEAST WITH MY WET CLOTHES AND ALL. FIRST THING WE GOTTA DO IS . . .
. . . BUILD A FIRE.

HMM. MAYBE THERE AREN'T ANY WOOD ELVES LIVING INSIDE YOU. NO SELF-RESPECTING WOOD ELF WOULD EVER TURN DOWN A DELICIOUS TREAT!
TYSON'S BELLY HURT BAD, DOCTOR!

SOME OF THIS STUFF LOOKS LIKE IT'S BEEN IN HERE FOR YEARS. TALK ABOUT YER SLOW DIGESTION!
CERTAINLY TAKES THE CHILL OUTTA THE AIR.
I FEEL BETTER ALREADY!

AH! A NICE, ROARING FIRE! BUT Y'KNOW? SEEMS LIKE SOMETHING'S MISSING. . .
HEY, BIG JOHNSON! LOOK WHAT I FOUND!

WHY, THAT'LL DO RIGHT NICELY!
!
LET'S HOOTENANNY! YEEEE-HAW!
STOMPITY STOMPITY

TYSON'S TUMMY ON FIRE!!
WHOA! FIRE SPRITES! THAT'S BAD!
PURRTTT!

OW! OW!
PLEASE, MY PRINCE -- YOU MUST BE SEATED IF I AM TO COMPLETE YOUR PHYSICAL EXAMINATION!

BELLY HURTS!!
MY BABY!

WHIMPER...
WAIT! LISTEN!
HERE'S A LITTLE DITTY I COMPOSED IN MY SALAD DAYS -- WHEN I THOUGHT THE TRAVELING MINSTREL LIFE MIGHT BE THE LIFE FOR ME . . .

BLANG!
BLANG!
TYSON GETTING... ...URP... ...SICK!
SHE'S A SWEET, LITTLE, SWEET LITTLE TART, WHOMS I CALLS MY LITTLE SWEETHEART!
MUSIC-MAKING PIXIES! IT'S WORSE THAN I THOUGHT!
WHOO!
BLANG!
UUULG..

OH, MY.
HE'S GOING TO HURL, ISN'T HE?
HUURRK
HONEY, COVER YOUR MOUTH!

JUST AS I SUSPECTED! TRY TO HAVE A LITTLE FUN, AN' THEY KICK YOU OUTTA THE JOINT!
HANG ON! HERE WE GO!

URLLLCH!
MY BABY!
COVER YOUR MOUTH! A PRINCE ALWAYS REMEMBERS TO COVER HIS MOUTH!
MOM! DAD!
HOT!
HOT!
FOOMP
SPLASH!

UGH.
JOHNSON! THERE'S THE QUEEN! GET HER!

NO...
NO HURT MOMMY!!

STAY AWAY FROM MY MOMMY!
C'MON, BLOSSOM! I GOT AN IDEA!
HEY!

WHAT IN THE WORLD ARE YOU DOING?! WE'LL BE KILLED!
IT'S JUST LIKE WITH THE TWISTER, MR. PEEP! IF YOU CONTROL TH' RUDDER, THEN YOU CONTROL TH' BEAST!

AND EVERYBODY KNOWS THAT THE POWERS THAT BE PUT TAILS ON BEASTIES JUST SO'S I COULD USE 'EM FOR RUDDERS!
YEEE HAW!
LOOK OUT!

TYSON TAKE CARE OF AMPHIBIANS ONCE AND FOR ALL!
JUMP!

CHOMP!
GASP!

ooh!
HE BIT OFF HIS OWN TAIL!
OUCH!
UH, OH! I THINK HE'S GONNA FAINT!

ORG! ME NOT FEEL SO GOOD...
RUN!
LOOK OUT!
AAAH!

oooh!
AAAH..
WHAM
AAH!
ARG!

EVERYBODY OKAY? EVERYBODY I CAME HERE TO RESCUE, I MEAN?
WE'RE OKAY, BUT MOST OF THE RAT CREATURE ARMY IS UNDERNEATH TYSON!

MY BABY! MY BEAUTIFUL BABY'S TAIL!! WHAT HAVE YOU DONE, YOU - - YOU MONSTER?!!
WHAT DID I DO TO HIM? HEY, HE ATE ME!

WHY, YOU LITTLE RUNT . . . YOU'VE CAUSED NOTHING BUT TROUBLE SINCE YOU GOT HERE.
WELL, YOU MIGHT BE ABLE TO GET THE TAIL OFF OF AN INNOCENT CHILD. . .

BUT YOU WOULDN'T DARE TRY THAT WITH THE QUEEN OF THE RAT CREATURES!
SAY, THAT'S A MIGHTY FINE PELT YOU GOT THERE, MA'M . . .

SKREEE
SKREEEE
SKEEEEEE
ARE YOU SURE YOU HAVE TO GO, BIG JOHNSON?

NOT THAT IT AIN'T BEEN NICE, LILY, BUT IT'S A BIG OL' WORLD OUT THERE -- AND SOME OF IT I STILL AIN'T SEEN. I FIGURED I BEST GIT GOIN' BEFORE THE SNOWS COME.
BUT WHO'LL PROTECT US IF YOU LEAVE?

WHY, STILLMAN GOT HIS FLAME BACK -- HE'LL PROTECT YA! RIGHT, STILL?
I SUPPOSE. AT LEAST UNTIL THE DRAGON FROM THE HIGH COUNCIL ARRIVES TO CHOOSE MY REPLACEMENT.

YOU'RE TOO HARD ON YOURSELF, LITTLE BUDDY. SO YOU LOST CONTROL OF THE SITUATION -- WHAT, TWO, THREE TIMES? SIX TIMES TOPS -- BUT YOU BROUGHT IT BACK WHEN IT COUNTED...

I RECKON WHEN THIS HIGH AN' MIGHTY **DRAGON** FROM TH' COUNCIL SHOWS UP, **HE'LL** PICK THE RIGHT DRAGON TO GUARD THIS PLACE.

GOOD-BYE.
FAREWELL, CREATURES OF THE VALLEY! I SHALL NOT FORGET YOU AND THE EXPERIENCES WE SHARED -- FOR AT LEAST ANOTHER **FIFTEEN MINUTES!**

THERE HE GOES.
MAYBE SOMEBODY ELSE WISHED ON A STAR AND HE HAS TO GO AND HELP THEM NOW.

I THINK HE WAS RIGHT ABOUT **YOU**, STILLMAN! YOU HELPED US ESCAPE FROM THE **PANTRY**, AND YOUR FLAME KEPT THE RATS BACK UNTIL **BIG JOHNSON** COULD HELP US!
BUT WHAT IF BIG JOHNSON **HADN'T** SHOWN UP?
THE RATS WOULD HAVE OVERRUN THE VALLEY AND THE ANIMALS IN YOUR CHARGE WOULD'VE BEEN EATEN.

NOW **HOLD IT** RIGHT THERE! I **DID** GET MY FLAME BACK, AND WE WERE PUTTING UP A PRETTY GOOD **FIGHT** --

YEEEEK!
THE DRAGON FROM THE **HIGH COUNCIL!**

I'M SO SORRY, GREAT SON OF MIM, PLEASE FORGIVE ME FOR BEING SO STUPID. IT'S JUST - - IT'S BEEN A ROUGH COUPLE OF DAYS AND. . . .
DON'T SWEAT IT.

I KNOW WHY YOU'RE HERE AND I WHOLEHEARTEDLY AGREE WITH THE HIGH COUNCIL'S DECISION TO REPLACE ME AS THESE ANIMALS' GUARDIAN.
REPLACE YOU? WHY? IT LOOKS LIKE ALL THE ANIMALS IN YOUR CHARGE ARE SAFE AND SECURE.

BUT I DIDN'T. . . . IT WASN'T ALL BECAUSE OF ME . . .
OF COURSE IT WASN'T. BUT THAT'S HOW IT WORKS, ISN'T IT? STILLMAN, FIRE-BREATHING DRAGON, I OFFICIALLY APPOINT YOU TO BE THESE ANIMALS' GUARDIAN.

I . . . I . . . I WON'T LET YOU DOWN, SIR!

THOSE RATS BETTER BE CAREFUL NEXT TIME! WE'LL TEACH 'EM THAT WE'RE NO PUSHOVERS! WE'LL SHOW 'EM WHO'S BOSS!
I THINK YOU'VE ALREADY DONE THAT.

YOU MEAN IT? REALLY?
YES . . .

. . . I THINK YOU AND YOUR FRIENDS LEFT QUITE AN IMPRESSION. . .

LOYAL SUBJECTS, IT IS OUR DARKEST HOUR SINCE THE PASSING OF OUR BELOVED KING. . .
AS YOU ARE ALL AWARE, SOMETHING OF GREAT IMPORTANCE HAS BEEN TAKEN FROM US - - SOMETHING THAT DEFINED US - - THAT SET US APART AS THE MOST ATTRACTIVE CREATURES OF THIS VALLEY!

COUGH!
HACK.
I'M TALKING ABOUT OUR TAILS. MY BEAUTIFUL SON WAS THE FIRST TO SUFFER THE LOSS - - AND I SOON FOLLOWED.
BAD BAD BIG JOHNSON AMPHIBIAN!

A STRANGER TO OUR VALLEY - - THE BIG JOHNSON BONE - - FIRST USED OUR TAILS AS HANDLES, THEN TO OUR GREAT DISGRACE - - HE TOOK THEM FROM US!!

THE QUEEN AND HER ROYAL SON, BOTH NOW MISSING THEIR MOST DELICATE AND BEAUTIFUL OF APPENDAGES - - WHAT WAS A QUEEN TO DO?

AND HOW WOULD IT LOOK FOR THE QUEEN AND PRINCE TO GO ABOUT TAIL-LESS, WHILE THEIR SUBJECTS CONTINUED TO WALK ABOUT- - THEIR TAILS TWITCHING SEDUCTIVELY IN THEIR WAKES? NOT TOO GOOD I TELL YOU!
AND SO I HAVE AN ANNOUNCEMENT TO MAKE!

NEVER AGAIN SHALL OUR OWN TAILS BE USED TO HUMILIATE US! NEVER AGAIN SHALL OUR OWN TAILS BE USED AS WEAPONS AGAINST US!

A ROYAL DECREE IS HEREBY MADE! HENCEFORTH, ONCE A YEAR ALL RAT CREATURES UNDER THE AGE OF ONE SHALL BE GATHERED BY THE TRIBE AND THEIR TAILS CUT OFF! THIS DAY SHALL BE CALLED - -
- - TAIL-CUTTING-OFF DAY!

AS FOR YOU ADULTS, WELL . . .
. . .YOU ALREADY KNOW WHAT SACRIFICE I HAVE ASKED OF YOU.
HOORAY FOR QUEEN MAUD! YAY!
SIGH.

I'D LIKE TO THANK EACH AND EVERY ONE OF YOU FROM THE BOTTOM OF MY HEART FOR THE GREAT SACRIFICE MADE IN THE NAME OF OUR PEOPLE AND FOR BEING SUCH GOOD SPORTS. THANK YOU, AND GOOD NIGHT!
HOORAY FOR YOU, QUEEN MAUD!
HOORAY FOR ALL OF US!

SO LET ME GET THIS RIGHT -- YOU GOT SUCKED UP BY A TORNADO AND DROPPED IN A VALLEY FILLED WITH DRAGONS AND GIANT RATS --

-- AND THEN THE QUEEN OF THE GIANT RATS FED YOU TO HER SON?!
HAW! HAW!
THAT'S A GOOD ONE, MISTER!
THAT'S RIGHT! AN' I HOOTENANNIED IN HIS BELLY 'TIL TH' BEASTIE PUKED ME UP!
THEN I STRUCK IT RICH BY FINDING A GIANT NUGGET O' GOLD! WHICH I USED TO BUY THIS HERE PROPERTY AND BUILD M'SELF A TRADING POST. AIN'T THAT RIGHT, MR. PUP?
Wood
Rope
Jerky
Pickles
SIGH. YES.
HE SAID, LET'S BUILD A TRADING POST AND YOU CAN RUN IT, HE SAYS. I'D RATHER DROWN IN A PUDDLE OF MY OWN SPIT, I SAY.

THOSE ARE SOME MIGHTY TALL TALES, LITTLE MAN.
I HOPE YOU DON'T EXPECT ME TO BELIEVE . . . 'EM.
BELIEVE WHAT YOU WANT, SIR, BUT I'M OFF --

THE SIREN SONG OF ADVENTURE IS A-CALLIN' ME AGAIN!

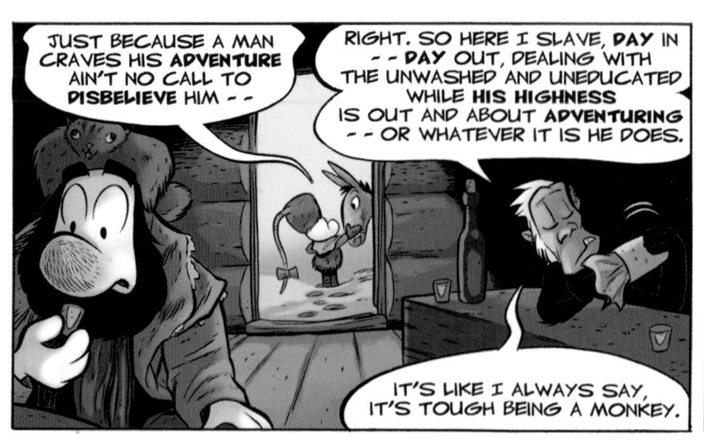
JUST BECAUSE A MAN CRAVES HIS ADVENTURE AIN'T NO CALL TO DISBELIEVE HIM - -
RIGHT. SO HERE I SLAVE, DAY IN - - DAY OUT, DEALING WITH THE UNWASHED AND UNEDUCATED WHILE HIS HIGHNESS IS OUT AND ABOUT ADVENTURING - - OR WHATEVER IT IS HE DOES.
IT'S LIKE I ALWAYS SAY, IT'S TOUGH BEING A MONKEY.

- - BIG JOHNSON BONE IS A MAN OF HONOR - -

IF ANY PART OF MY STORY AIN'T TRUE, MAY THE POWERS THAT BE DROP A FULL SEASON'S WORTH A SNOW ON MY HEAD RIGHT NOW.
BIG JOHNSON DON'T STRETCH TH' TRUTH!

WELL, MAYBE ONLY JUST A LITTLE. LET'S GO, BLOSSOM, GIRL.
THE END

Z-
!
WOW! WHAT A WEIRD DREAM I JUST HAD ABOUT BIG JOHNSON BONE AND THE QUEEN OF THE RAT CREATURES!
GOSH! I WONDER IF IT WAS BECAUSE I WAS WEARING THE BIG HAT?

The End!
JEFF SMITH

QUEST FOR THE SPARK

BOOK ONE

Return to the amazing world of *BONE* in Book One of the brand-new trilogy written by Tom Sniegoski and illustrated in full color by Jeff Smith.

Turn the page for a special sneak peek!

A weakened sun dawned feebly in the eastern sky, its golden rays trapped by ominous gray clouds. There wasn't the slightest chance of sunlight reaching and warming the Kingdom of Atheia far below.

Gran'ma Ben awoke with a start, that terrible gitchy feeling that made her head swim and her legs wobble rousing her from a restless sleep. This wasn't good — not good at all.

She'd had this feeling off and on for most of her life, the first time when she was just a little girl and Princess of Atheia. She later became Queen, but then she gave up the crown to move to the Valley and raise her granddaughter, Thorn.

There's nothing worse than starting a day off with the gitchy feeling, she thought, throwing back the covers and pulling on her robe against the chill that filled her bedroom. It was an omen of bad things to come. She could spend the whole day just waiting for something to happen, and it always did. The gitchy feeling was never wrong.

And this time, Gran'ma didn't have long to wait.

She stood in front of the window in the royal castle, the damp wind tousling her white hair, and took note of the heavy sky. That was when she heard the scream, high pitched and filled with fear.

Gran'ma Ben tore from her room out into the castle hallway, eyes squinting through the early morning dimness as she searched for the source of such a horrible sound. The scream came again, and she found herself growing afraid as she ran toward it, for the scream was coming from the royal bedchamber.

From Queen Thorn's room.

Not bothering to knock, Gran'ma Ben threw open the door and charged inside. The Queen's handmaiden, Prissy, stood beside the large bed, her eyes wide and swollen with terror.

Queen Thorn lay in the center of the grand mattress, the sheets and blankets rumpled at her feet.

"What is it, Pris?" Gran'ma asked.

"I heard her cry out," Prissy said, her voice trembling. "I thought she was having a nightmare."

Queen Thorn, held firmly in the grip of sleep, moaned as her head thrashed from side to side upon her pillow.

“Looks like she still is,” Gran’ma Ben said. She reached down to gently grab hold of her granddaughter’s foot. Her toes were cold, like pieces of ice.

“Thorn, honey, wake up.” She gave the girl’s foot a shake. “It’s all right, you’re having a bad dream. . . . Time to wake up.” The Queen moaned all the louder, whimpering pathetically.

“Thorn?” Gran’ma called again, raising her voice. She squeezed the girl’s toes enough to hurt.

But still the Queen remained asleep.

“Do you see?” Prissy asked in a frightened whisper. “I tried to wake her, too . . . but she won’t wake up.”

Queen Thorn groaned and began to tremble with what could have been the cold, or something worse.

This was the kind of thing that Gran’ma Ben had always been afraid of, the kind of thing that she had hoped to protect her grandchild from when she’d whisked her away to hide in the Valley. But fate had a way of tracking you — like a bloodhound on a scent — and it found them, disrupting the peace that they’d had for so long.

Gran’ma reached down to the foot of the bed and pulled the covers up and over her sleeping grandchild, just as her own head began to swim and her legs began to wobble again.

It was an omen of bad things to come.

And the gitchy feeling was never wrong.

BOOK ONE

In the Quest for the Spark adventure you'll meet:

TOM ELM, a turnip farmer's son from the Valley who just might be destined for something greater. . . .

PERCIVAL F. BONE, explorer extraordinaire who loves the smell of adventure – and has a pretty cool airship!

BARCLAY AND ABBEY BONE, Percival's nephew and niece who can't seem to get along – or stay out of trouble.

RANDOLF CLEARMEADOW, a former Veni Yan warrior who still knows his stuff. . . .

And don't forget Gran'ma Ben, Queen Thorn, the two stupid, stupid Rat Creatures, and Roderick the raccoon, who are all back from the original *BONE* series!

Coming February 2011

About JEFF SMITH

JEFF SMITH was born and raised in the American Midwest and learned about cartooning from comic strips, comic books, and watching animated shorts on TV. After four years of drawing comic strips for The Ohio State University's student newspaper and cofounding Character Builders animation studio in 1986, Smith launched the comic book *BONE* in 1991. Between *BONE* and other comics projects, Smith spends much of his time on the international guest circuit promoting comics and the art of graphic novels. Visit him online at www.boneville.com.

About TOM SNIEGOSKI

TOM SNIEGOSKI is the author of more than two dozen novels, including The Fallen, a teen fantasy quartet that was adapted into an ABC Family Channel miniseries, and the Billy Hooten: Owlboy books. With Christopher Golden, he coauthored the OutCast series, which is in development as a film at Universal. Sniegoski was born and raised in Massachusetts, where he still lives with his wife and their Labrador retriever. Visit him online at www.sniegoski.com.